DOCTO

GW00788021

Dr Lorna Marsden joins Matthew
Thornton's general practice determined
never to become involved with her
employer. But with Dr Thornton's
cynical views on love and marriage,
surely she's in no danger of that?

DOCTOR'S ROMANCE

BY

SONIA DEANE

MILLS & BOON LIMITED
15–16 BROOK'S MEWS
LONDON W1A 1DR

First published in Great Britain 1985
by Mills & Boon Limited

© Sonia Deane 1985

Australian copyright 1985
Philippine copyright 1985

ISBN 0 263 75082 5

Set in 10 on 12pt Linotron Times
03–0685–52,100

Photoset by Rowland Phototypesetting Ltd
Bury St Edmunds, Suffolk
Made and printed in Great Britain by
Richard Clay (The Chaucer Press) Ltd.
Bungay, Suffolk

CHAPTER ONE

LORNA MARSDEN said to herself, 'I couldn't tolerate working with this man, even though he is recognised as one of the best physicians in Tetbury. He's austere, severe, dominating, and far too handsome. Being his assistant would be like working with an iceberg.' In short, Dr Matthew Thornton infuriated her.

At that point he said firmly, 'Well, Dr Marsden, do you want the job or not? I haven't any time to waste. You've seen the practice quarters, met Mrs Keen, my secretary-cum-receptionist . . . this is a very specialised practice and there'll only be the three of us.' He paused, faintly impatient. 'You've gone over all the preliminaries, and you know exactly my requirements.'

Lorna flashed him a critical stubborn look. 'I'd like a little more time to think it over.'

'I haven't any more time,' he said sharply, 'but I have other applicants. I want an answer.' His attitude was forbidding and challenging.

Lorna struggled, fought, and despising herself, surprisingly capitulated.

'Very well . . . I'll join you.' It was as though he had mesmerised her into making a decision through the sheer force of his personality. Lorna was vital, vivacious, but could be both quiet and calm. Her grey-green eyes reflected every shade of emotion and could soften in sympathy, or flash in anger and defiance. There was a challenge in her attitude, and strength in her character.

At heart, she was romantic and adventurous, and her slim body hinted at sensuousness, giving her an irresistible fascination. She had come to Tetbury wanting to get away from London where she had trained.

Unexpectedly, even shatteringly, Dr Thornton gave an infectious chuckle, his features creasing into an indulgent, broad smile that transformed his expression.

'I didn't mean to brow-beat you,' he said, half-apologetically.

'Then you gave a good impression of doing so!' she flashed back. A smile hovered on her lips as she relaxed.

'The possibility of having to interview another applicant drove me to desperation,' he admitted. 'And it's been one of those days. The death of a special patient; the alcoholism of a ne'er-do-well; and a sad miscarriage.'

Lorna studied him with increasing interest, ignoring her first adverse reactions. She suspected that working with him would be like running the gauntlet, but, at least, never dull. He was tall and broad-shouldered, and had an air of importance without conceit. His strong features suggested authority, while his eyes were perceptive and disarming; eyes that assessed without betraying their verdict and had an inscrutability that was part of his charm. An element of mystery about him suggested hidden power. He was respected by colleagues and patients alike, while retaining a certain reserve which, to some degree, isolated him from the social life of Tetbury. No one gossiped about Dr Thornton—if anything, they stood a little in awe of him; a fact which strengthened his influence.

'I know what you mean,' she said with understanding, 'and I'm sorry about the loss of your patient.'

'He was a good friend. Thirty-five . . . coronary.' He hurried on to avoid emotion, 'And you live here, in Tetbury. I wonder we haven't met.'

'Actually,' she said, 'we have. At the Fabians' twenty-fifth wedding anniversary.'

'William and Jill,' he exclaimed immediately, warmth in his voice.

'They're only acquaintances of mine,' Lorna admitted. 'I met them through Dr Elliot.'

'Now let me see,' Matthew Thornton temporised, picking up her letter of application from his desk. 'You have been working for Dr Elliot in Malmesbury until a few weeks ago.' He hastened, 'I know Hugh Elliot socially, but only *of* him professionally.'

'He's moving to London,' Lorna volunteered. 'The lure of Harley Street. My being with him was ideal for me, seeing that Malmesbury is only about six miles from here.'

'I shall be on your doorstep.'

'Which could be *too* near!' Lorna laughed.

'Not since you'll be doing the night calls,' he pointed out.

'That's what assistants are for,' she said, and they smiled.

There was a hardening of his features as he said, 'This practice isn't a bed of roses. The area's pretty scattered.'

'All the more challenging.'

'You like challenge?'

'Yes; one gets in a rut otherwise, and sinks into soggy medicine, always reaching for a prescription pad as an easy option: tablets and more tablets.'

'You'll do, Lorna,' he said. 'And I haven't any time to dance around the formalities—I'm Matthew.' He held out his hand. 'Shall we seal the bargain—not under protest,' he said with a disarming smile.

His grip was firm and she was aware of his touch beyond the symbolism. Faint annoyance ruffled her because only a matter of minutes before she had been convinced that she couldn't tolerate working with this man and now, here she was, won over by his undoubted charm.

'Not under protest,' she agreed.

'Can you help me out almost immediately? I'm desperate.'

His voice when used without aggression, she thought, faintly ridiculing herself, would persuade anyone that black was white. She had never met a man quite like him before, and the prospect of working for him quickened her heart-beat and brought a sudden unexpected excitement.

'I'd be happy to begin tomorrow,' she said honestly.

'Splendid . . . do you live with your parents?'

'No, alone.'

His brows raised slightly.

'My father's an accountant, and he and my mother live in London. I love Gloucestershire and came here rather in defiance of their wishes. My godmother left me Sunset Cottage and I was determined to live in it.'

He studied her somewhat unnervingly. 'You would not easily be deflected,' he said at last.

Lorna laughed. 'No,' she admitted. 'However, once I'd settled here, they discovered the advantage of having a country retreat for the week-ends, and all is harmonious. They're darlings, really, and I can't stand friction.'

'Neither can I.'

'But, equally, you do not suffer fools gladly,' she observed.

'I can be very impatient,' he warned her.

'And icy,' she dared to say.

His gaze was exploratory and inescapable.

Lorna glanced down at her hands which were clasped in her lap; colour mounted her cheeks, as emotion swept over her.

'And icy,' he conceded. 'Probably a defence mechanism!' His voice dropped and echoed into the silence, holding her in its spell. How old was he? Thirty-two or so. And had his Fellowship. Dr Matthew Thornton FRCP. She felt instinctively that he would be meticulous when it came to his patients. Did he own Gable's End, the house in which she now sat? It was a solid, yellow Cotswold stone building, standing in a small garden. Now, in October, the trees were splashes of flame and gold, their tints burnished by the autumn sun which had a warmth often lacking in summer. She glanced up at the high ceiling of the consulting room and at the attractive oak beams; white walls and a wood-block floor, set off a rich red carpet and a few discreet antiques, giving it a friendly atmosphere balancing the clinical appearance of the instrument cabinets. She noticed his casual grey suit and immaculate white shirt which he wore with careless ease.

'Well,' he asked, 'do you approve of it all?'

She said half-apologetically, 'I was just thinking how attractive it is. So different from the usual utility, soulless consulting room.'

'Patients always have problems,' he said, 'and I think the right atmosphere is important. I work better in the right environment, too. There is no virtue in shabbiness and discomfort. It isn't a matter of money; some people would make an orange box with a cloth on it look better than others with valuable furniture.' He gave a disarming half-apologetic smile. 'All doctors talk too much, given half a chance.'

'Probably because they are trained to listen.'

'And you'll come in tomorrow,' he said abruptly and irrelevantly, seeking reassurance.

'Promptly at nine, or earlier if you wish.'

'We have appointment surgery which begins at eight-thirty,' he said dryly. 'By the way, I'd like you to take over the Duty Doctor slot on some Saturdays. I've warned you it isn't a bed of roses, but I prefer to work without partners as long as I can.'

'Which tells me,' she said boldly, 'that it is useless my hoping to become one.'

He contemplated her thoughtfully before saying frankly, 'Not at the moment; but I haven't a crystal ball for the future.'

Lorna wasn't perturbed. She loved her work and, while ambitious, valued the satisfaction of a job well done rather than the acclaim that went with it. She asked herself if she was not too content with her life and its pattern. Her colleagues had warned her against leaving London, inferring that no one was ever ill and nothing ever happened in the country!

The telephone rang at that moment and an agitated voice cried, 'Oh, Doctor; the lady I work for, she's that ill . . . You know me, I'm Mrs Nilson—you look after my daughter, Mrs Cook, and my grandson . . . It's Miss Anson; can't stop being sick . . . If you could come . . . I'm scared. It's Cornerways, a mile out of Tetbury on the Malmesbury road; can't miss it. Responsible I feel, she's new here and on her own.'

'I'm on my way,' Matthew said reassuringly, and put down the receiver. 'Can't afford to ignore a call like that,' he mumbled. 'I know Mrs Nilson's family . . . Does the name Anson mean anything to you?' He was picking up his medical bag as he spoke.

Lorna shook her head. 'Afraid not. Can I be of help?' There was a note of eagerness in her voice.

'By all means,' he said. 'May be nothing, but—' He shook his head, 'One never knows.'

They went out into the warmth of mid-October. Tetbury lay in a golden haze, its wide streets and ancient Town Hall (once a spacious Market Hall standing on pillars) dominating the centre of the town, exuding the atmosphere of a past glory, when the wool trade had flourished and the merchants' fine houses—some still preserved—bore testimony to its importance. Today it stole the limelight because of the proximity of Highgrove House, the residence of the Prince and Princess of Wales.

They found Cornerways, a grey stone building standing back a matter of yards from the road.

'Looks lonely,' Lorna said.

'Perhaps it is,' Matthew observed cryptically.

A plump healthy-looking country woman, with rosy cheeks, answered the door to them.

'Oh thank you for coming, Doctor . . . I'm that relieved.'

'Hello Mrs Nilson; this is my assistant, Dr Marsden . . .'

'Miss Anson,' the woman hurried on, having nodded to Lorna, 'hasn't been here very long, you see. Only got the place straight last week. Been looking that *ill*, hasn't eaten nothing, just dragged herself about.'

'No relatives?'

'Only a mother as I know of, and she's in some foreign place, not expected home until after Christmas. Miss Anson paints pictures, lovely pictures. *Sells* them, too,' she added proudly, her enthusiasm overtaking anxiety as she led the way up the long winding staircase. Now that 'the Doctor' was there, all would be well. She lowered her voice, 'I told her you was coming, after I spoke to you,' she added in a confidential whisper.

Felicity Anson lay back against the pillows looking a putty grey; emaciated, hollow-eyed. Her long flaxen hair was in disarray, and as she saw Matthew and Lorna she murmured, 'So *ill*, so sorry . . . to trouble you . . . don't know *why*.' She heaved unproductively in a violent body-racking spasm.

Matthew made a thorough examination, brows puckered, and when at last he drew up the bedclothes, said quietly, 'You're pregnant.'

She stared at him stupefied. *'Pregnant!'* It was a gasp.

'And you're ill,' he added gently. 'It's essential we get you into hospital immediately.'

But the patient was on the verge of fainting.

'You look after her,' Matthew said to Lorna, 'while I telephone.' He spoke as though he and Lorna had been associated for years, and had a complete professional understanding, which even in that moment, Lorna recognised.

A little wail came as Lorna placed a cold damp towel (obtained from the adjoining bathroom) at the back of Felicity Anson's neck.

'We'll soon have you better,' she soothed.

A hand groped for hers. 'Don't leave me . . . *please* don't leave me.'

Lorna realised that here was a girl normally striking, with high cheek-bones and a pale fine skin—a classic type of beauty. Age about twenty-four, now looking twice that.

Matthew returned. An ambulance would be there as quickly as possible. Mrs Nilson packed a small case.

Panic and desperation sapped the last remnants of Felicity Anson's strength as she was eventually transferred to the stretcher, and she cried out to Matthew and Lorna not to abandon her, and leave her just to the hospital staff who would all be strangers.

'*We* shall come to see you, and you will be in the hands of a friend of mine,' Matthew promised.

'I've no one,' came the weak, forlorn, half-apologetic whisper. 'I'm not married.'

Matthew and Lorna stood in silence for a second beside his car after the ambulance had driven away. Around them the countryside glowed in the beauty of the evening light. Even in that moment of drama it struck Matthew that Lorna had a radiance about her; that her dark lustrous eyes were full of compassion; that the curve of her red lips suggested gentleness and sympathy, also that her sensuality was part of her personality. Infinite relief overwhelmed him because he knew intuitively that he had found the ideal colleague, who would be popular with his patients as well as being excellent at her job.

'I was lucky enough to be able to speak to Mr Leigh Warren,' he explained.

'Mr Margrave's registrar,' Lorna said immediately.

'You know him?'

'I've talked to him on the telephone. Dr Elliot and Mr Margrave were friends.'

Matthew smiled, opening the car door and seeing her into her seat. She looked up at him and again was overpowered by his attraction and the subtle charm that was completely effortless. Despite this, there was no hint of any deliberate attempt to charm. She breathed deeply, determined never to become involved with an employer, knowing it to be the surest way to disaster. Either it led to a torrid affair, or to unrequited love, or to the ultimate wrecking even of friendship. From detesting this man during the first moments of assessment, she now sought to establish a solid foundation on which to build a successful, and platonic, association. There was nothing whatsoever flirtatious in his manner—no long significant looks—merely a disarming friendliness.

'What's the prognosis in Miss Anson's case?' she asked as they drove away from the house.

'Possible termination. We shall seé. Something appealing about her,' he added involuntarily. 'There's always a story,' he added. 'And doctors hear more than most.' He put the car into gear and shot off, breaking a short silence by asking, 'Did you mind my suggesting that we look in on her a little later?'

'Not at all. I'm not doing anything.'

'And it's my free evening. Dr Hadwell—Guy Hadwell—and I have a reciprocal arrangement . . . do you know him, too?'

Lorna shook her head.

'You'd like Guy; all women do,' he added easily.

It was impossible, Lorna thought, to put this man into any category. His inscrutability was contradicted tantalisingly by a disarming frankness.

'That is my cue to say that I'm not "all women",' she countered.

He shot her a speculative glance.

'I'm inclined to agree with you.' He added, 'I can't see you easily losing your head over anything.'

'Or anyone?' Her tone was provocative.

'That, too. I think you would go in for sustained assessment.'

She laughed. 'You're probably right. Hospital training, perhaps.'

'Keeping the wolves at bay,' he suggested.

She felt his mood change; a fixed, solemn expression clouded his face as he said irrelevantly, 'We'll give them an hour or so, and then see how things are. Can I drop you at—?'

'I've to collect my car from Gable's End,' she reminded him, laughing.

'Of course! You left it there. How stupid of me.'

'Are you usually so concerned about your patients—I mean, beyond giving them the benefit of your advice and professional skill?' There was a degree of surprise in her voice.

He stiffened, and retorted a trifle curtly, 'I don't consider that my responsibility to Miss Anson ends merely by my getting her admitted. She needs the back-up of her own doctor. I seem to be cast for the role since she is new to the district. All that will have to be gone into when she's in a fit state to discuss it.'

Lorna felt rebuked, aware that he would not take kindly to having his motives, or his actions, questioned.

About an hour-and-a-half later, Lorna met him at The Royal Hospital on the outskirts of the town. He was well-known and greeted cheerfully by the nursing staff. It struck Lorna that this was the first time she had actually visited a patient in the company of that patient's doctor. It was very different when she was part of the hospital staff herself. Now she was conscious of walking with Matthew down the corridors of an intimate building, viewing the sick without being responsible for their care. There were anxious relatives with hunted eyes losing their way in the labyrinth; the grieving and the bereaved, making up the medley of human beings isolated by their misery, bravely concealed in most cases. The smell of ether and disinfectant; trolleys rumbling; doors swinging, leading to mysterious secret worlds.

Matthew went into Sister's office in private wing. She was an attractive Welsh woman of about thirty, efficient, but human, with a much appreciated sense of humour. He introduced Lorna swiftly and didn't waste time on superficialities. 'Miss Anson?' he asked.

Mr Leigh Warren joined them in that moment.

'Ah, Matthew,' he said immediately, 'the Anson case.' He flashed Sister an understanding look before adding, 'Hyperemesis Gravidarum. Her condition's serious, just as you thought. She's dehydrated, her blood pressure's dangerously high.'

'Termination?' Matthew uttered the word as a question.

'Yes. Mr Margrave's going to do it. I'm on my way to theatre now. No time to lose.'

Matthew nodded. 'I'll ring later,' he said.

They looked at each other in understanding. Leigh Warren, a cheerful-faced, slightly podgy young man, popular with patients and colleagues alike, hurried away.

'I wonder how she will take it,' Lorna said as she and Matthew left the hospital. 'When it's all over.'

'Ah! That's another story,' he said significantly.

When next they saw Felicity Anson, the following evening after surgery, she was lying back against the pillows, wan, abject, her beauty emphasised despite her pallor. Lorna had a sudden uncanny presentiment that this girl was destined to play an important part in her life; that their paths were irretrievably linked.

'How are you feeling?' Matthew asked with solicitude.

'Fragmented,' she admitted without self-pity, but poignantly. 'There was no time to take it all in, and now there's a strange hollow feeling of—of *loss*.'

'There was no alternative,' he assured her.

'I know. I couldn't have gone on as I was. The relief of not being sick and feeling so *ill*—' Her voice broke and tears of weakness gushed to her eyes. 'You have been so kind—so understanding. Thank you, Dr Thornton, for leaving that message which I got when I came round. It meant a great deal to know that you and Dr Marsden were coming this evening.' She looked from face to face and put out a hand towards Lorna; the gesture more expressive than words.

And all the time she spoke, Lorna was aware that she was studying Matthew with an intent, almost speculative gaze, as if there was a question she wanted to ask him, but lacked the courage to do so.

'You're the first artist I've ever met,' he said, wanting to introduce a different note. 'Amateurs, yes.'

Felicity Anson sighed. 'I've commissions piling up . . . work has been impossible.'

Would she, Lorna wondered, confide in them; fill in any of the details of her life?

But she rushed on, 'They say I can leave here in a couple of days, then I'll have to—' Again her voice broke. 'Everything seems so unreal at the moment.'

Lorna watched Matthew surreptitiously. What was he thinking? It was impossible to tell from his expression, yet she felt strongly that he would not have been sitting there unless he were emotionally caught up beyond the mere concern of a doctor for his patient. There was just something in his manner that awakened faint apprehension. But what had it to do with her? Why have any reaction to his behaviour?

'Work helps,' Matthew said gently. 'Trite, but very true.'

She nodded, averting her gaze, struggling not to cry.

'Could we—could we meet again?' she asked jerkily. 'I mean—'

'You must come and see my crazy cottage,' Lorna put in quickly. 'Not an even floor in the place.'

'I'd like that.'

Matthew said, 'I shall certainly keep an eye on you . . . and now we must be going.'

'Oh!' It was a little weak sound of wistful appeal rather than an exclamation. She looked like a distressed child about to be abandoned, but she forced a smile as she murmured, 'Thank you both, again.'

Leigh Warren and Staff came in at that moment, and Lorna felt that Matthew was relieved to be able to escape from a situation that upset him.

A tall, bronzed, smiling man hailed them as they reached the entrance lobby.

'Hello, there!' He addressed Matthew and then

looked with a deepening interest and open admiration at Lorna. 'Would you be the new assistant?' he asked hopefully, continuing to hold her gaze.

'She would,' Matthew confirmed, making the introduction.

Guy Hadwell, Lorna thought. *The man all women love!* Now she understood why. He was very attractive in a relaxed fashion, his features betraying a good temper and sense of humour. He also had a glint in his eyes that betrayed his liking for women.

'Matthew has all the luck,' he said cheerfully. 'Welcome to the club! We're a happy, harmless bunch, grateful for feminine glamour to add a spot of interest . . . What are you doing here?' he addressed Matthew.

'Seeing an emergency patient.'

'Do I know him, or her?'

'A Felicity Anson.'

There was a sudden tense silence.

'The artist?'

'Yes.'

'Good lord!' The words came with embarrassed amazement.

'You know her?'

Guy looked awkward.

'She's pretty well-known,' came the evasive reply. 'Didn't *you* know of her?'

'No; but, then, I'm not really up in the art world.'

'Is she ill?' The question concealed anxiety.

'No; minor operation,' Matthew replied discreetly.

Lorna was aware of the unease and reticence in Guy's manner.

'Then that's all right,' came the somewhat feeble comment. 'Must rush—friends coming for drinks and

I'm late.' He looked straight into Lorna's eyes. 'I'll ring you sometime if I may,' he added decisively, and his expression of interest intrigued her.

Matthew made an impatient sound as Guy left, 'I ought not to have mentioned Miss Anson's name,' His tone was self-critical.

'I don't see that there's any breach of confidence there,' Lorna protested. 'You were talking to a colleague, after all, and someone who might well have to stand in for you sometime.'

'Nevertheless, I think the name mattered to him,' Matthew insisted. 'Don't you?' The question held suspense.

'That depends on what you mean by "mattered",' she replied.

'I didn't ask you for evasion,' he said somewhat impatiently.

'Very well, then,' Lorna flashed back, 'I think her name had importance far in excess of her fame. But why should anyone have to give chapter and verse about their relationships, either past or present?'

'A world of secrets,' he suggested, eyeing her, brows puckered.

'Of privacy,' she countered. 'Have you known Dr Hadwell long?'

'Only three years,' Matthew admitted. 'He took over the practice when his father died, and enlarged it. He now has two partners.' As he spoke, Matthew looked back down the corridor as though drawn in the direction of the room they had left. He said abruptly, 'Let's get out of here. I'm in no mood for emotional complications.'

When they reached the car park, he stood uncertainly

by his car. Lorna's was in the line immediately opposite. 'Come back for a drink,' he suggested persuasively.

Excitement touched her.

'I'd like to.' She had reached her car almost by the time he had opened the door of his.

They arrived at Gable's End within seconds of each other, and he led her into the house, hand on her arm without any deliberate gesture.

'Ah!' he exclaimed pleasurably as they went into the large, chintzy sitting room that held mellow family furniture. A large vase of Michaelmas daisies, golden-rod and dahlias, stood in an alcove, splashing vivid colour against the muted golds and greens of the carpet and hangings. An unmistakable smell of old books mingled with the faint fragrance of furniture polish and, much to Lorna's surprise, a fire burned in the Adam's fireplace.

'A *fire*,' she said with delight.

'You can't get any satisfaction from standing with your back to a radiator,' he said with feeling. 'But we've got central heating as well as. Fires are coming back into fashion, and even if they weren't, I'd still manage to have one somehow!'

He was, Lorna thought, an amazingly contradictory man, and there was a whimsical, almost puckish defiance about him as he took up his position with his back to the flames, hands flicking up his jacket.

'You want the best of both worlds,' she suggested.

'Guilty . . . Stay for supper. I told Mrs Cummings, my housekeeper, not to prepare anything special, but—'

'Thank you all the same, but I've things to do . . . I did rather tumble into the job!'

He crossed to the drinks tray. 'True—one's life can

change in twenty-four hours . . . What can I give you?'

'Dry sherry, please.'

An extraordinary sensation stole over her as she took the glass and looked up at him. It was as though she had been there many times before, and that she had known him for years instead of days. His manner suggested acceptance without conflict, and a determination to meet her on her own terms, without creating any sexually orientated atmosphere. And while she was completely relaxed, her feminine contrariness subconsciously rebelled at the absence of sensuality. It struck her, nevertheless, that he could be the type who, once emotion was roused, would be both powerful and passionate.

'Those are absorbing thoughts,' he suggested.

She started, slightly embarrassed.

'I was thinking that it seemed as if I'd been here many times before.'

He smiled at her, his expression pleasurable.

'No strangeness, thank heaven. We don't have a great deal of leisure, so that to spend it with people with whom we are not in harmony is sheer waste of time.' He changed the subject smoothly, 'By the way, how did you get on with Mrs Richards this morning?'

'Anti-husband syndrome.'

'Ah!' satisfaction oozed from him. 'So you spotted that.' He added honestly, 'I can never make out whether the aversion to sex came before the husband, or the other way around. And they are in their mid-thirties.'

Lorna said sagely, 'She'd not had any experience before she married.'

'She never admitted that to me,' he exclaimed, surprised. 'Amazing, these days, how self-conscious women are about virginity. In the old days they were proud of it.'

'Be that as it may, it comes down to the fact that the right contraceptive would help,' Lorna spoke with emphasis.

He made a helpless gesture. 'I've tried her with everything.'

'But you haven't applied the same rules to the husband.'

Matthew looked slightly startled. 'You mean a vasectomy?'

'Yes; it would prove that he cares about her point of view *and* physical difficulties, and was prepared to do something about it.'

'Pretty drastic.'

'Why? Because it's the man? I don't hear any protests when it's tubal ligation—sterilising the *woman*.'

'A point,' he conceded.

'She needs a little whiff of romance; he's been only concerned with the purely sexual satisfaction angle, indifferent to all the adverse reactions she's had with the pill, the coil, the progesterone injection—but, then, you know . . . but you don't *understand*.'

'Thank you,' he said wryly. 'You're right, of course. That's why I handed her over to you.' He laughed. 'You came just in time. In fact I've been searching for you for a very long while.'

Lorna felt a thrill of satisfaction. 'Women *do* appreciate women's problems.'

'The voice of experience.' His gaze was intense and interested.

'Not in the way you infer, but I can well imagine what irregular periods, and all the disadvantages that go with

them, must mean in a marriage.' She paused and then
added deliberately, 'Incidentally, I happen to be a vir-
gin, but I'm neither self-conscious, nor apologetic,
about it.'

'I've no answer to that,' he said with a smile and, a
short while later, took her glass. 'Just a small one before
you go, and you'll be well within the driving limit . . .
Reverting to the Richards' problem, I can see you've got
to grips with it. Has *he* agreed to see you?'

'Yes; tomorrow.'

'Excellent . . . marriage should be re-drafted. Highly
charged emotion doesn't stand fire.' His voice was
resolute, emphatic, almost aggressive.

'I haven't time to discuss that,' she countered.

He looked at her with directness. 'We'll make time
one day,' he announced forcefully. But even as he
spoke, a strange, almost haunting sadness crept into his
eyes.

'A hobby-horse of yours?'

'Perhaps,' his voice was low and subdued. He changed
the subject abruptly, 'Do you think Felicity Anson will
pick up the threads of her life without too much trauma?'

Lorna sighed. 'That rather depends on where the man
fits into the picture.'

'The man,' he commented ruefully, 'is all too often
absent.' He added a little self-consciously, 'I'd be glad if
you'd keep in touch with her. She needs someone, and
you're just the right person.'

Lorna made a grimace. 'I don't know if I like that!
Makes me sound like an Aunt Sally!'

'On the contrary, it makes you a perceptive, sympathetic girl, who knows how to handle people.'

'Marginally better,' she said.

'And you can't be persuaded to stay for something to eat?' he queried as she got to her feet.

'Thank you, no.' She didn't want any precipitate relationship.

'Stubborn, too!' he said.

'Decisive,' she corrected.

They smiled at each other, and he walked with her to the front door, standing outlined in the moonlit darkness after seeing her to her car. He was an impressive figure and at that moment a little mysterious, his pleasant expression concealing his thoughts rather than betraying them.

Lorna drove the short distance through the silent empty town, the flower baskets hanging around the Market Hall, pricked out in the moonlight. A sense of space and antiquity created an atmosphere of peace and old-world charm. She wound her way down Silver Street until she came to her cottage which was tucked out of sight. It had four rooms, bath and kitchen, and carriage lamps served to sustain the atmosphere of the past, despite the electricity, shining on oak beams and polished wood floors, which were adorned by rugs. She had inherited the contents of the cottage which boasted one or two antiques, and a carved Jacobean wall-cupboard filled with valuable china. A large copper cauldron stood in the deep chimney corner, and bellows and a warming pan hung on the side beams. Logs were already stacked ready for igniting. A royal blue carpet covered the stairs and landing, bringing the scene to life, while leaded windows looked out on a small court-yard containing a miniature rock-garden, wedged between black-and-white Tudor buildings. The thought of Matthew became almost visual, and she decided to invite him for a meal one evening. The future suddenly held promise, and a wave of happiness brought excitement.

It was ten days later when Guy Hadwell telephoned her.

'I know you're just going to start surgery,' he began, 'but I haven't your home telephone number.' He spoke with confident ease, as though his contacting her was taken for granted. 'How about having dinner with me at The Apostle Spoon this Saturday?'

'In Malmesbury,' she said, startled, but not averse to the idea.

'Yes . . . sorry it's such short notice.'

Lorna replied spontaneously, not allowing her surprise to show, 'Thank you; I'd like that.'

'Tell me where you live and I'll pick you up.'

She told him.

'Then about seven; and I'm known for being punctual—as punctual as a doctor can be.'

'Which,' she joked, 'isn't saying much!'

'Seven,' he laughed, and rang off.

Matthew came into her consulting room at that moment. She was holding the receiver in her hand and staring at it as if it were animate, a puzzled half-smile on her lips. She said naturally, while conveying a degree of surprise, 'That was Dr Hadwell inviting me to dinner on Saturday.' She waited for Matthew's reaction.

There didn't appear to be one as he commented, 'Really? I gather you accepted.'

'Yes.' She met his gaze. 'How did you know?'

'By your intrigued expression,' he answered smoothly. 'We've got a full surgery.'

She nodded.

He said, lost to the mention of Guy, 'I'm seeing Mr Richards—as you know.'

'Yes; he wanted to deal with you when it came to the details.'

A sudden inexplicable aggression and abruptness made Matthew's voice harsh as he said, 'That's understandable; but I'm so tired of all this cloying romantic nonsense which causes so much upheaval and tragedy in marriage.' There was a strong note of disgust and impatience.

Lorna tensed. It struck her uneasily that she knew nothing whatsoever about his life; that he had never volunteered any information about himself, his background, or his parents. Nor—apart from Guy Hadwell—about his friends. She looked at him questioningly. Just then he seemed almost austere; a man in shadow, resistant to any intrusion in his private world. It wasn't a matter of curiosity, or prying into the past, but of establishing a degree of familiarity linked with human interests. She said impulsively, 'Would you like to have supper with me this evening—see my cottage?'

He avoided her gaze for a second and then said politely, 'Thank you, but I have a load of paper-work to get through . . . some other time, perhaps.'

Just then she heard the echo of his words, '*The cloying romantic nonsense which causes so much upheaval in marriage*', and realised that he appeared to have a cynical contempt for anything to do with emotion, while contradictorily, being a sensitive and sympathetic man towards any form of suffering. Nothing added up, which was increasingly disconcerting.

When she said good-bye to him that evening, he was sitting at his desk, and called her name when she had almost shut the door on her way out of the room.

'Yes?' There was anticipation in her voice.

But all he said was, 'Mr Richards is going into the Sunberry Nursing Home for his operation tomorrow. He thought it was a major job, instead of no more than having a tooth out.'

'Between us,' Lorna suggested, 'we have at least achieved something.'

'You tackled the problem with far deeper insight than I,' he admitted.

'Thank you.'

Lorna watched him as he moved the papers on his blotting pad and then returned to what appeared to be his letter writing. He nodded vaguely and she went from the room.

Back at the cottage, after a meal, she decided to drive over to see Felicity Anson. When she arrived at the house and was about to turn into the drive, to her amazement she saw Matthew's car parked there.

CHAPTER TWO

LORNA saw Matthew's car with a degree of shocked surprise. Why couldn't he have been honest about the visit, since it was obviously the reason for his refusing her invitation to supper? Instinctively she swung the car away from the drive and raced back towards Tetbury as though being followed. She was critical of her own annoyance, insisting that Matthew's actions had nothing whatever to do with her, and that if he preferred to spend the evening with Felicity instead of her, that was his business! Nevertheless the following morning she waited half-expectantly for his confidence, looking at him in anticipation after the rush of surgery was over, and casually bringing Felicity's name into the conversation.

Matthew met her gaze with calm detachment and said, his thoughts apparently elsewhere, 'By the way, I'd like you to examine a Mrs Read this morning . . . do a smear test. She's a nervous little woman and you'll know how to deal with her.'

'Thank you.' Lorna's voice was crisp. 'Does that comment mean that she's about forty; fussy, and inconsequential?'

'Good lord no; why?'

'Because your description implied—'

'My description,' he said testily, 'was precisely right. Mrs Read is nervous; and she's about five feet two.'

'You make it sound patronizing,' Lorna said.

'And you sound as though you got out of bed on the wrong side . . . something upset you?'

She flushed, furious with herself. 'Can't I make a comment?'

'If it's intelligent . . . I've a long list of visits between surgery. And a midder hanging fire.'

'Induction?' She tried to be conciliatory.

'Prefer not. It's the first. A honeymoon baby.' He smiled indulgently.

All Lorna could think of were his words about the 'cloying romantic nonsense' which he believed caused so much upheaval in marriage. 'I shouldn't think that even the honeymoon would appeal to you,' she said, 'let alone the baby!'

'We were not discussing me,' he retorted icily, turning on his heel and striding to the door. 'And I suggest you improve your frame of mind before seeing any more patients.'

When he'd gone, Lorna clenched her hands and let out an explosive, 'Damn!', furious with herself.

Matthew's description of Mrs Read turned out to be apt. She *was* a nervous little woman, who entered the consulting room tentatively, her expression anxious. She had bird-like features, a pale complexion inclined to sallowness, which lack of make-up emphasised. Her bluey-green eyes were dull, but kindly. She was 'neatly' dressed in a sombre navy coat and matching dress, handbag, shoes and gloves.

'I'm very worried,' she began, 'but so grateful you are here. Oh,' she hurried on, 'Dr Thornton is very nice, but I'd much rather have a lady doctor. You see, I transferred from one when I moved to Tetbury from

Chippenham. My husband retired . . . I've got to be examined, haven't I?'

'That's nothing to worry about,' Lorna said reassuringly, thinking that Mrs Read had the hallmark of an old-fashioned spinster, rather than a wife.

'Dr Thornton mentioned a cervical smear, but they do that when they suspect *cancer*.' Her voice was fearful.

Lorna said with emphasis, 'We do it for precautionary and diagnostic reasons so that we can deal with anything that might be wrong. Now,' Lorna smiled encouragingly, 'just you go in there—' She indicated a changing-cubicle which was off the examining-room. 'Call me when you're ready,' she added in friendly tone.

Mrs Read darted to the door like a rabbit to a burrow.

'Well?' Matthew asked after evening surgery was over.

'How about Mrs Read?'

'There's cervical erosion; we'll know more when we get the result of the smear test.'

'Let's hope you only need to cauterize her.'

Lorna nodded. 'Her husband is considerably older than she, and she obviously married late.'

'So she implied,' Matthew said.

Lorna exclaimed, 'You weren't patronising.' Her voice was half-apologetic.

'I should hope not,' he protested vigorously. 'She *is* a nervous little woman, but I should judge her to be a pleasant one.'

'That is my impression, too.'

'Then we agree on something!' He looked forbidding.

Lorna wanted to stimulate the suggestion that they agreed on most things, although she realised that there was self-delusion in the idea.

'You don't like people to disagree with you?' she challenged.

'On the contrary, I'll accept anything that is valid.'

'Valid according to *your* standards.'

'Naturally. I can't make judgments for others.' He studied her carefully. 'You're in a contrary mood, Lorna.' He added, 'I don't like moody people—they're boring. You know where you are with an explosive temper that's over and done with. So, if you've got anything to say, any grievance, out with it. Or,' he paused imperceptibly, 'if you suffer from pre-menstrual tension, warn me, and I'll duck!'

His directness appealed to her, and she said laughingly, 'That's the last thing—and I agree with you about the moods . . . I'm sorry I've been a bore,' she added, the word having stung.

'I'm not arguing with you.' His tone was that of dismissal.

Silence fell which he broke after a few seconds by saying, 'I'd like you to be on duty this coming Thursday, by the way. I've a dinner engagement.'

She nodded and murmured her agreement. But she couldn't help wondering if he was taking Felicity out. It also struck her that, despite the ease with which she had settled into the practice, and his attitude generally, it was obvious that he had no intention of widening their horizons, or becoming more intimately involved. She said impulsively, 'Saturday evening will be all right, won't it?'

'For what?' He looked vague.

'I'm having dinner with Guy Hadwell and—'

His expression was blank as he said, 'Yes, yes, of course. Glad you reminded me.' He added, 'Keep your fingers crossed that this midder comes off before then!'

She flashed back, 'Before Thursday, too.'

He sat down at his desk. 'I see what you mean; yes, certainly before Thursday, too.'

Lorna exclaimed involuntarily, 'Don't tell me that you are going to work this evening.'

'No—why?'

Lorna thought better of making reference to his pretence at working the previous evening.

'I'll lock up,' she hastened, and as she left him she felt that he had vanished into some private world. A little bleak sensation stole over her.

Back at the cottage, she piled more logs on the newly-lit fire, showered, and decided she would luxuriate in her house coat and have supper on a tray. Outside, October was screaming to a close as the wind got up and howled as though resenting the closeness of November. Its burnished leaves still hung tenaciously to many trees, and fog hung over the valleys. It was colder than normal, emphasising the comfort and warmth of the now fiercely burning fire which glinted on copper and brass. Lorna sighed with satisfaction. And just as she was about to start eating her quiche, the doorbell rang and set every nerve in her body tingling because, absurdly, the name that came to mind was Matthew's. But to her amazement, Felicity stood there, wrapped in a sable coat that added to her striking beauty.

'I've no right to be here,' she began, 'but—'

'Come in,' Lorna said welcomingly. 'Yes, I am having supper, but that doesn't matter. And you'll forgive my house coat.'

'It's a very beautiful house coat,' Felicity exclaimed.

admiring the quilted red satin sashed garment which was far more attractive than many dresses.

'Warm,' Lorna said with a smile.

'This is perfect,' Felicity murmured as she reached the sitting room and saw the fire. 'What a picturesque cottage, and how beautifully you've arranged it all!'

Lorna took Felicity's coat and indicated an armchair opposite her own. Felicity's being there didn't seem in the least strange.

'How about a brandy?' Lorna moved towards the drinks tray, her expression persuasive. 'I shall have one when I've finished eating—'

'I'd love one,' Felicity agreed. 'It's so *cold* out, and we notice it after the little warmer spell . . . I just wanted to talk,' she rushed on, 'and I remembered your invitation.'

'I'm glad.' Lorna poured out two brandies and they settled in their respective chairs, Lorna finishing her quiche and taking the tray out to the kitchen. There was no hypocrisy in her attitude to Felicity. She liked her instinctively, and was intrigued by her life as an artist, as well as the facts that had recently emerged. The firelight flickered over her delicate features and bone structure, giving her pale skin an almost translucent look, and as Lorna studied her she felt a pang, not of jealousy or envy, but as one might feel when watching a beautiful piece of sculpture.

'I wanted you to know a little more about me; you were so kind—oh, far more than you realise. An *attitude* is so important. I didn't have time to take in the full implication of the situation . . . you and Matthew made the path so smooth.'

Matthew! The name on her lips made Lorna start.

'That is what doctors are for,' she insisted.

Felicity's slim body relaxed and seemed to be moulded in her chair as she went on, 'There was no tragedy, no unhappy love affair involved in my being pregnant. The father of the child wasn't important to me. It had been just one of those things—a midsummer madness, if you like. We met at a house party . . . and we were both so *happy*—the giving kind of happiness that bubbles up for a short while, and carries one along with it.' Felicity cupped her hands around the brandy glass and leaned forward as she spoke, looking intently at Lorna. 'Can you understand that?'

'I think so,' Lorna said softly, and had cause to remember those words later on.

'I'm not promiscuous,' Felicity said honestly. 'I had a lover from whom I parted amicably. So far as the father of the child is concerned: he had no idea I was pregnant, any more than I had. I shall never tell him—no good purpose would be served, and it is most unlikely that I shall ever see him again.' She gave a relieved sigh. 'I feel better for having confided in you.'

Lorna could not resist the question, 'May I ask if you told Matthew, also?'

Felicity shook her head. 'Matthew isn't the kind of man to want emotional confidences outside his professional role, or to betray his own emotions. It would be very difficult to judge what he is thinking . . . Do you like working with him?'

'Very much.' Lorna sipped her brandy, put down the glass, and threw another log on the fire which spluttered and sent up sparks of blue flame, indicative of the frost. She both wanted to talk about Matthew and, contradictorily, shrank from doing so. 'He is a very fine doctor.'

'Everyone spoke very highly of him at the hospital, and the nurses gave him almost a film-star image which he would hate. I can just imagine him cringing if I were to tell him! Strange, I feel I know quite a bit about him—' She hesitated.

Lorna cut in, 'Which is surprising, since you just said that it would be difficult to judge what he is thinking.'

'Woman's intuition perhaps,' Felicity replied without guile. 'He's the one person who makes me wish I could sculpt *people* instead of things. He would make a fine subject.'

Lorna asked abruptly, 'Why?'

'Because there's a dark mystery about him . . . Oh, nothing sinister! A question of secrecy.' As she spoke Felicity looked directly into Lorna's eyes with questioning intensity, as though willing Lorna to confide any knowledge in her possession. 'Haven't you noticed that he never talks about himself?'

Lorna said discreetly, 'When one is working, there is very little time to go in for analysis, or even observation.' She paused, adding, 'In any case, I think we all have a private world into which we retreat on occasion.'

Felicity's expression changed to solemn reflection. 'That is very true. This is a lovely room, so welcoming and relaxing . . . Does Matthew—'

The doorbell made them both jump. Lorna answered it with a degree of impatience. Then, '*Matthew!*' she cried.

'My midder's over,' he said gleefully. 'Quick. No trouble. I thought we might wet the baby's head.'

'Felicity's here,' she said, wondering if he already knew.

'Really.' A smile hovered on his lips.

Lorna watched him carefully as he went into the sitting room and greeted Felicity without, she noticed, shaking hands. It was a free-and-easy greeting as of old friends meeting without formality being needed.

'Not a very pleasant night to be out,' he exclaimed. 'Freezing hard. You'll have to be careful driving home; the roads are icy in patches.' His concern and protectiveness were marked.

Felicity laughed. 'Is that the doctor talking, or the friend?'

'Both. I want a peaceful night.'

'We're having a brandy,' Lorna said easily, avoiding any mention of the midder since she didn't know how Felicity felt about the loss of her child. The impression conveyed was that the event had hardly borrowed even a facet of reality, since the knowledge and termination were simultaneous.

'Fine.' Matthew looked around him. 'This is splendid,' he exclaimed with enthusiasm, 'and I love those carriage lamps and the chimney corner—' He paused before adding, 'And *you* seemed surprised because *I* had a fire!'

'You haven't been here before?' Felicity sounded surprised.

'Too busy,' Lorna put in, and flashed him an enigmatic smile. 'The Doctor's Alibi!'

Matthew might not have heard. He followed Lorna to the drinks tray and helped himself as she indicated. She was conscious of his nearness and moved away, aware that his presence brought the room to life, and that even in a matter of minutes he had stamped his personality on it. But, like a film superimposed on the scene, was Felicity's intense interest, her inquiring gaze of assessment, as though she were endeavouring to find some clue which would enable her to know Matthew better.

'I suppose doctors are people we seldom really know,' Felicity remarked, regretting the fact, while actually wondering what Matthew's private world, as Lorna called it, embraced.

Matthew's laugh was low and attractive.

'Probably because they hardly know themselves! Too caught up with everyone else's problems.'

'I hadn't thought of that.' She looked solemn.

'You don't want to give us too much importance,' he said, smiling at her with warmth and indulgence, but there was an underlying note of warning in the remark.

'I second that,' Lorna exclaimed stoutly. 'We get far too much publicity these days. 'Although the women are not glamorised nearly as much as their male contempories,' she added caustically.

'There speaks women's lib,' Matthew announced critically.

'Nonsense,' Lorna protested.

Felicity said, 'You don't approve of women's lib, Matthew?'

Lorna looked from face to face. It seemed difficult to believe that Felicity and Matthew had become so friendly within such a short space of time, and she wondered who was instrumental in fostering the relationship since, from what she, herself, knew of Matthew, it was out of character.

'I dissociate myself from it,' he said smoothly. 'Women have a right to please themselves. I have a right to associate with women of my choice, and if they do not include the banner-waving, strident types, that's my business!'

'And Lorna and I are not that type,' Felicity teased.

'God forbid!' he cried, raising his eyes in horror. He added with satisfaction, 'Anyway, when the libbers get to us, they become merely *patients*. Nothing can change *that*.'

There was a momentary silence which Felicity broke by saying in a slightly nervous, self-conscious manner, 'By the way, Matthew, I meant to tell you last evening that I know your friend Guy Hadwell.'

Lorna flashed Matthew a faintly cynical smile which gave the meeting significance.

But he ignored it as he said, 'Guy . . . *really*?' There was interest in his voice.

'My mother and I knew him when he was in London. He traced me, and looked me up the other day.'

Both Matthew and Lorna wondered why Guy had given them the impression that he merely knew *of* Felicity, the artist, rather than Felicity, the friend, or acquaintance, and recalled that there had been an air of mystery in his attitude.

'Small world,' Matthew said briefly.

Felicity seemed about to enlarge on the matter, and then added somewhat irrelevantly, 'Have you lived here long, Lorna?' The words sounded flat.

'A few years.'

'I'm sorry I bought Cornerways . . . I don't particularly like the house. This has character.'

'But is small,' Lorna pointed out. 'You need space for a studio—all kinds of things.'

'True.' A wistful expression crept into Felicity's eyes.

'I have a genius for doing the wrong thing at the wrong time . . . But that's another story, and I must be going.'

'I must get back, too,' Matthew put in.

Lorna felt that a great deal had been left unsaid through Matthew's advent. But the spark of interest in the conversation seemed to have died at the mention of Guy Hadwell's name, and Matthew had done little to sustain further conversation.

Felicity asked a final question, 'Do you know Guy very well?' She addressed Matthew.

Matthew's reply was non-committal, 'We're colleagues.'

Felicity flashed Lorna a meaning smile, 'Not a very illuminating statement.'

'But true,' Matthew said. 'Obviously we're friendly, but the words "very well" imply a great deal.'

'And you never commit yourself,' Lorna said.

'I deal with facts,' he commented infuriatingly.

Their gaze met for a brief second. There was a hint of challenge, even of conflict, between them.

Lorna watched him as he got up from his chair, wishing that he would remain; but it was obvious he had no intention of doing so.

'Come again,' Lorna said to Felicity.

'I will,' came the enthusiastic reply.

Matthew helped Felicity into her luxurious fur coat, and she lifted the collar, smoothing it against her cheeks with a graceful gesture, her face peering above the soft dark fur like a flower. The lamp-light fell upon her features, on her expressive eyes that seemed full of secrets.

Lorna saw them to the front door.

'Now for the icy blast,' Matthew warned. 'Winter has arrived prematurely and with a vengeance.'

There was no moon, but the light from the cottage illuminated their cars, and the road flanking the cottage shone as though polished. The cold cut into their faces as Matthew took Felicity's arm protectively, and then looking back at Lorna, cried, 'Don't stay out here—you're not dressed for the part!'

Lorna shivered and shut the door, then went to a window and watched as they stood talking for a few seconds, their breath discernible in the frosty air. She sighed as she let the curtains fall back into place and heard the cars drive away. The cottage seemed suddenly empty and, in some strange way, its restfulness had gone. In that moment life reminded her of the scattered pieces of a jigsaw puzzle without a picture. Felicity's attitude towards Matthew was difficult to describe, she thought, as she returned to her chair by the fire. Not possessive, but disarmingly natural. She was not flirtatious, but might already have staked her claim to a part in his life. And what did time matter when it came to the progress or intimacy of human relationship? Had Guy Hadwell been the lover from whom she parted amicably? And what did that matter, either? Lorna glanced at the grandfather clock that ticked away in the silence. It was only ten o'clock. The logs tumbled one over the other, spurting into a blaze, throwing shadows across the beamed ceiling and flickering over a copper jug filled with autumn leaves and flowers. She looked beautiful as she sat there; a vibrant, almost provocative beauty, her large eyes eager for life and full of expression. Emotion touched her, sending a shiver over her slender body. Every nerve seemed sensitised; her awareness of her surroundings acute, making her solitude almost an affront. She got up restlessly. She had visualised Matthew coming there for the first time, and this evening had been an anti-climax. Impatient with herself, she turned out the lights and went to bed. Her last conscious thought queried whether Matthew's Thursday evening appointment was with Felicity.

'You have a most attractive cottage,' Matthew said the following morning, meeting Lorna's gaze with obvious approval. 'It has atmosphere. I liked it.'

'I'm glad. I must say I thoroughly enjoy it.'

'And won't want to leave it when you marry,' he suggested with a wry smile.

They became aware of each other in that second, and she said in a breath, 'That will not be for a long while. I'm certainly not in any hurry to marry.'

'That sounds aggressive!' His gaze didn't move from her face. 'Tomorrow has a knack of confounding our theories or intentions.'

'That depends on how decisive we are.' Her voice was full of resolve.

He shook his head as though giving up. 'You're in a strange mood, Lorna.'

'Yesterday, according to you, I was both moody and boring!'

'Which proves my point.' A half-smile hovered on his lips. 'Interesting that Felicity knows Guy. I thought—well, we both thought, that there was something in his manner when he spoke of her that evening—something mysterious.'

'Known as discretion,' Lorna suggested. 'A doctor's second name.'

Matthew gave a short laugh.

'True . . . Well, I've got that midder off the list,' he went on as though nothing else was important; then becoming unexpectedly grave, he added, 'but I'm up against a tricky case this evening—the daughter of friends of mine. Not exactly intimate friends, but we have drinks together from time to time, and I go to most of their celebrations. They have two children—boy of eighteen and girl of about sixteen, all patients. Clare, the girl, is much older than her years, and looks it. She rang me this morning and wants to see me—without her parents' knowledge.'

'Oh!' Lorna looked apprehensive. 'Contraception?'

'Quite probably—if we're lucky. One doesn't have to be Sherlock Holmes to assume that the problem will be sexual. She is sophisticated and headstrong . . . I'd like you to meet her and have your opinion. She rang me from a call box.'

'I'll be around. What time is she coming?'

'Seven this evening. She's at Highbanks, hopefully on her way to university; but, of course, she can't get away during school hours.'

'Do you get many cases in her age group?'

'Too many; and they're on the increase. And I've a nasty feeling that Clare Wayne isn't going to be easy.'

'Whatever it is, you'll deal with it,' Lorna said confidently.

He brightened. 'Think so?'

'Certain.'

Lorna stayed on after surgery and admitted Clare Wayne who gasped, 'But I came to see Dr Thornton.'

'That's all right,' Lorna assured her. 'I'm Dr Thornton's assistant. He is ready to see you.'

'Oh!' Clare added, confused, 'Stupid of me to expect him to answer the door!'

Clare looked at least eighteen, and was extremely attractive in a striking, rather bizarre, fashion. Her dark hair was fashionably unruly and she threaded her fingers through it as she jerked back her head in a nervous gesture. She had an air about her of one accustomed to getting her own way, and even being at a disadvantage didn't eliminate it. Nevertheless Lorna knew that her confidence was evaporating, and she paled as they made their way to Matthew's consulting room.

Matthew greeted her with a welcoming smile, shook her hand, and then indicated the patients' chair.

'Now,' he said encouragingly, 'what's the trouble? Work; boy friends?'

She undid her coat and threw it back and, avoiding his gaze, said with a trace of defiance, 'Irregular periods.'

Matthew didn't believe her, but exclaimed, 'Nothing to worry about in that. Common in a girl of your age.'

She stared him out and regained a little of her lost confidence.

'Friends of mine have been put on the pill—it's effective, isn't it?'

Matthew said directly, 'Are you asking me to pre-scribe a contraceptive, Clare?' His voice was firm.

She looked confused. 'Not exactly, but—'

'Unless you're honest with me I cannot help you.' He looked at her very levelly. 'You were most insistent that your parents should not know about this visit. Why?'

'Parents fuss,' she temporised. 'I didn't want a lot of discussion and, anyway, I'm old enough to manage my own affairs without running to them—' She stopped, knowing that she was not being convincing.

'And now,' Matthew said quietly, 'suppose you stop wasting my time. You're afraid you're pregnant.'

She cried, 'No,' and again, '*no!*' And suddenly the defiance vanished as she whispered, 'Yes—oh, yes.'

'Then,' Matthew said gently, 'we must make sure.'

'But my parents mustn't know; they *mustn't* know!'

'Suppose we deal with one thing at a time?' he suggested. 'When was your last period?'

'I've missed two . . . but I am irregular.'

'Then this may well be a false alarm.'

She brightened, and her voice lowered to a note of apology, 'I know you must think badly of me and—'

'I'm your doctor, not a judge, Clare. I'm here to help you no matter what the problem. And if there *is* a problem, then we've got to tackle it.'

Tears gushed to her eyes. 'You're very kind . . . I didn't know what to expect and—'

Matthew flicked down the intercom and asked Lorna to come in.

'I'm going to examine you,' Matthew said easily, 'and Dr Marsden will help you—she's my assistant.'

'Oh . . . People often miss periods without being pregnant, don't they?' Courage returned in the wake of hope.

'Often,' Matthew assured her.

Lorna came in, led Clare into the changing room, and then saw her on to the examining couch.

Matthew made a thorough examination. The breasts were tender; the uterus soft and enlarged.

'Any morning sickness?' he asked.

'Only twice, and I felt faint; but I had been to a late-night party the night before,' came the swift reply

'Are you passing water more frequently?'

Clare's eyes widened with fear. Her, 'Yes,' came in a whisper.

Matthew drew up the covering blanket and said quietly, 'There's no doubt that you're pregnant. Get dressed and we'll talk.' He returned to his room.

Clare looked stunned. She clutched Lorna's hand. 'Couldn't he be wrong . . . I mean . . . I can't *have* it. He's *wrong!* He *must* be wrong.'

'Not when all the symptoms are positive,' Lorna said, her expression both understanding and sympathetic.

Clare seemed to have shrunk in a matter of minutes. Fear, stark and absolute, stripped her of the poise, the sophistication, the confidence. She dressed in a kind of frantic disorder, dropping garments, stumbling, her heart thudding, her mouth dry. When she reached Matthew's consulting room she flopped down in the chair like a lifeless sack, her eyes wide and appealing as all she could say was, 'I'm not going to *have* it, and if you won't help me, I'll find someone else who will.' The spark of defiance returned to restore a little of her spirit 'If you won't think of me, think of my parents. They're your *friends*.'

Matthew ignored that as he asked, 'The man, Clare. I want to know the circumstances.'

Emotion, fright, cowardice made her rap out, 'He doesn't come into it. Why waste time talking about *him*?'

'Because since you've decided to live like an adult, I expect you to behave like one now. I'm not here to moralise; neither do I terminate pregnancies because they are inconvenient. On the other hand, circumstances have to be taken into account. I shall want you to see a colleague of mine—'

'I won't see anyone,' she almost shouted, control vanishing, 'and if you tell my *parents*—' Her eyes blazed.

'And how do you think your parents would feel if they knew you were facing this crisis without trusting them enough to take them into your confidence?'

She interrupted him, 'I don't want to hurt them, but can't you see that I don't *want* the child, anyway. What would I do with a child? And, what's more, I shouldn't want it if I were older and *married*.' Her voice was hard and scornful, her expression bitter. 'And I wouldn't marry its father even if he were free—which he isn't. Now you'll be even more horrified, I suppose.'

Matthew said evenly, 'Doctors are never horrified, or surprised; and marriage is the last thing I'd advocate.' His voice lowered to a note of gravity as he looked up from her case notes, 'And you are not yet sixteen.'

'I shall be at Christmas,' she insisted defiantly. 'And it's no good your asking me the name of the man, either. I may not want to marry him in any case, but I wouldn't betray him.' She looked at Matthew boldly. 'Well! You know all the facts! Are you going to give me an abortion or not? You know that's why I'm here.'

Self-control vanished; the wildness and self-indulgence that was part of her make-up took precedence over reason, courage, or consideration for others. She was beyond caring what Matthew thought of her. He represented salvation; escape from the consequences of her actions, and denied the possibility of those benefits she became a virago.

'I want you to see a colleague of mine,' Matthew said again firmly, 'before any decision is made I'll arrange an appointment for tomorrow.'

She made a little impatient gesture, 'So that you can

both assess the state of my mind and all that mumbo-jumbo. Make sure that I'd be mentally and physically harmed by having the child in the circumstances. Oh, I know the routine. I've read it often enough in the newspapers!'

'I don't want any argument, Clare. You will do as I say,' Matthew rapped out sternly.

'You could put me into a nursing home; pretend I'd got some minor ailment that would satisfy my parents—'

Matthew might not have been listening as he picked up the receiver and made an appointment with Alec Margrave for eleven o'clock the following morning, twisting his secretary's arm to arrange the consultation.

'And I suppose he's a psychiatrist,' Clare scoffed. 'The *last* thing I want. Listen, my parents are going away this week-end and I'm staying with a friend . . . I can easily think of something to tell *her* . . . You won't tell my parents I've been here?' she added, her mood swaying back to fear and pleading.

'*I* shall not tell them; but I wish *you* would.'

She raised her voice again, 'Not a chance. Never. Everyone's broadminded until it comes to their precious offspring.' Her eyes darkened in a mixture of fury and fear. 'I couldn't stand the "discussion", or their "understanding" and "being so good to me!" It would be sick-making.' She got up abruptly from her chair, dropping her gloves and forgetting her handbag as she turned on him fiercely, 'I didn't think you'd be so—so *sticky*,' she cried.

Matthew ignored that as he said gently, 'Be here at ten-thirty tomorrow morning and I'll take you to Mr Margrave. He's a very kind, understanding man.'

She stood there, half-child, half-woman; resentment

all-consuming. She wanted to be free from suspense and responsibility; to be whisked into a nursing home on some pretext at a moment's notice, so that she could forget the whole distasteful business. Just then she hated Matthew because he had thwarted her impossible aims. She rebelled at any vital formalities because, until now, everything in her life had been simple and self-satisfying.

'A problem there,' Lorna said, when Matthew returned from seeing Clare out.

He pursed his lips and shook his head. 'I'm afraid it would be dangerous not to terminate. We're dealing with an unstable character, spoilt, rebellious. When I think of her parents—there's so much at stake. They cherished the illusion that she could live life to the full in this modern world and still retain a set of values. They've given her freedom without licence; struck what appeared to be the happy medium.'

'Emotion doesn't recognise those words,' Lorna said adamantly, 'even though you do despise it.'

'My concern is how I'm going to discipline that emotion after all this is over,' he said shortly. 'There's more to consider than just a pregnancy. We come to the question: is contraception the answer? and, What are the parents' rights? Unless I can instil some kind of responsibility, even if based on fear—' He heaved a deep sigh and made a helpless gesture.

'This could scare her,' Lorna said hopefully.

He looked sceptical as he said, 'I hope you're right.'

And at that moment Clare was sitting in a café having coffee, fuming. All this *fuss*. But she'd win in the end. So Mr Margrave was kind, understanding. She would think out a plan of campaign to convince him that she was distraught, incapable of facing up to the future, and in no fit condition to have a child. That was *true*, she argued, but at least she'd triumphed in one direction: Matthew wouldn't tell her parents. Damn not being sixteen! She couldn't get a drink, and she couldn't drive a car. But, she thought furiously, she could become pregnant. Suddenly, unexpectedly, tears rolled down her cheeks while sobs tore at her, as fear and loneliness struck in a wave of terror.

CHAPTER THREE

LORNA was conscious of a certain suspense in the atmosphere when she greeted Matthew the following morning. He went through the day book, grunted at the sight of one or two names, and said to Lorna after she had opened up the surgery and was about to go into her room, 'I want to be away from here before six this evening. You can deal with any stragglers that sneak through the doors at the last minute, can't you?'

'Of course.'

'Damn,' he said, as the telephone rang. But his voice mellowed, 'Felicity! Of course not. Six . . . and you're sure you don't want to change your mind about having dinner out somewhere?' He laughed. 'I'm sure you can cook! Very well, I'll let you prove it! Until six—'

He put the receiver down. Lorna might not have existed and she hurried away, feeling self-conscious and dismissed. Surely, since she knew Felicity, he could have passed some comment, particularly in view of the meeting at the cottage.

Surgery dragged. Each patient had an appointment, and was given a number by Mrs Keen so that he, or she, was seen in strict rotation, and at the summons of a buzzer which rang in the waiting room. The cases were routine—colds, coughs, nothing that required much ingenuity. Half the time Lorna marvelled that people braved the elements when they could have dealt with their respective ailments at home. But, despite the

51

progress of modern medicine, there was, more than ever, a desire for a prescription of some sort, and a reassuring word from 'the doctor'. Lorna had already grown accustomed to the regulars of the 'never well' brigade, whose imaginary symptoms gave them an excuse for living at half-mast.

'Clare will be here at any minute,' Matthew said when he and Lorna met after surgery was over. 'I can't see Alec Margrave agreeing to a termination without the parents being put in the picture.' He sighed anxiously. 'Under-age cases like this are dynamite.'

'You'll do what is for the best,' Lorna assured him.

'I'm glad of your confidence. I need it.' He looked at her and said unexpectedly, 'Thank you.'

Lorna studied him with sympathetic understanding, thinking that few people ever imagined, or even considered, the stress involved for the doctor; the strain of decision-making and maintaining the confidentiality of the patient. Particularly when the finer points of the law had to be taken into account. 'Send for the doctor'; 'the doctor will know'; 'the doctor will help'. No one ever asked who would help 'the doctor'! It was all part of his job. Perhaps that was why the incidence of heart failure among them was greater than in any other profession.

Mrs Keen rang through on the inter-com. Miss Wayne had arrived.

'I must start my rounds,' Lorna said as Matthew went to the door of his consulting room.

'See you later.' He added, 'We might snatch a sandwich at lunch-time.'

'Good idea.' She knew that what he was saying wasn't registering; they were merely escapist words. But, to her surprise, when she returned to Gable's End after finishing her rounds, he greeted her and said, 'Sandwiches and coffee ready!'

'How lovely. November has certainly come in—' She didn't finish her sentence, but asked, 'Mr Margrave?'

'Agreed that there is a case for a termination, but the parents must be told. Clare has become the girl of fifteen—frightened, demented to the point where she will agree to almost anything to end the nightmare. She wants *me* to tell her parents.'

'And you will?'

'Gladly, with her consent. And human nature, Lorna, must always be taken into account. The fact that the problem is to be solved almost before Mr and Mrs Wayne have suffered through it, will enable them to bear Clare's defect with far more fortitude, no matter how great the shock.'

'That is very wise and cynical.'

'Wisdom, alas, too often has its roots in cynicism,' Matthew said ruefully. 'It is gleaned from mistakes, not virtues.'

'You should write a book of maxims!'

He laughed. 'I hate even writing a letter!' He handed her the sandwiches and took one for himself, devouring it as though he hadn't eaten for days.

Lorna said irrelevantly, 'I wonder if Dr Hadwell will mention Felicity when I see him on Saturday.'

'Is there any reason why he should?' Matthew countered tersely.

'No more than that she should have mentioned *him*,' Lorna said.

'I don't see that it matters,' he said on a note of impatience.

Lorna spoke with infuriating confidence, 'Anyway, I expect we shall all meet up before long.'

Matthew shot her a rather surprised gaze. 'You evidently assume that your relationship with him is likely to become permanent.'

'And you doubt he will wish for that?' The words rushed out.

'Nothing of the kind,' he snapped. 'And the subject isn't worth arguing about.'

Lorna asked herself if his irritation was due to jealousy of Felicity's friendship with Guy. Or the fact that he had no desire for a foursome, and was tacitly warning her.

'I wasn't arguing.'

He knocked his coffee cup over at that moment, the contents pouring over the occasional-table on which he had set it.

'Damn!' he said.

They looked at each other and burst out laughing.

'That will teach you to be so snooty,' she cried, using her table napkin to mop it up.

'Makes us even . . . No more coffee, thank you. I'm not looking forward to seeing the Waynes this afternoon.'

Lorna met his gaze. Words weren't necessary.

She noticed that Matthew changed that evening into a formal suit of grey, with a plain blue shirt and attractive silk tie which prevented any sombre note. As she studied him, Lorna's thoughts rushed back to Felicity's description—*'There's a dark mystery about him. Nothing sinister. A question of secrecy.'* The words seemed doubly apt. He stood there, tall, handsome and compelling; a man whose presence lingered long after he had gone from the room. A man difficult to dismiss from one's thoughts, and whose voice echoed intrusively in unexpected moments. The effortlessness of his attraction, his ease of manner, emphasised its power. It was obvious that Felicity was deeply interested in him, and *interested* seemed suddenly to be the right word. She seemed intrigued by the fact that his secrecy became a challenge, which Lorna felt Felicity longed to question. For all that, he looked grave and as though reading Lorna's thoughts said, 'It went off better than I'd hoped. Irene Wayne is a fine person.'

'Ah,' Lorna murmured, 'I was wondering about the Waynes.'

Matthew would never forget the look of distress on Irene Wayne's face when he told her Clare was pregnant. Or the compassion in her voice as she said, 'I *knew* there was something. I've been so worried, but I put her moods, explosive temper and sullen silences down to exams, school—anything to deceive myself, I suppose, although at her age pregnancy seemed . . . unreal, and so unlikely.'

Lorna prompted, 'And the father?'

'He wasn't there. I was glad. His wife will deal with him, and there'll be less trauma. Men don't stand up to these things with either the courage, or practicality, of women.' He glanced at his watch. 'And now to forget work, problems,' he said unguardedly, his expression and voice changing to bright anticipation.

Lorna envied Felicity the prospect of his company, although she wouldn't have admitted it.

'I'll give Mrs Leighton her injection tonight,' she said in a matter-of-fact tone.

'Good lord, yes,' he exclaimed. Then, 'If you would
. . . I don't think there will be many more needed.
Carcinoma of the lung . . .' He shook his head. 'A
devoted family—at least we've kept her as comfortable
as possible.' He drew Lorna's gaze to his in a con-
templative survey, behind which was gentleness.
'We don't have many periods of escape—do we?' he
mused.

'The patients are part of our life,' she said simply.
'And now you're going to another one!'

His expression changed as though a blind had been
pulled down between them. He turned, muttered,
'Good night, Lorna,' and left.

She stood staring after him, wondering what she had
said wrong.

Friday passed uneventfully. No word was said about
the previous evening. Lorna awakened on Saturday
morning in a mood of anticipation, and when Guy
Hadwell arrived to collect her at seven he might have
been a long-lost friend instead of someone to whom she
had hardly spoken. He brought an atmosphere of gaiety
with him and Matthew's words that 'women love Guy',
had a ring of truth. He admired the cottage, studied
Lorna in her simple, but smart, black-and-white jersey
dress, and said, 'You look very attractive, if I may say so!
Festive, too.'

'I feel it,' she admitted honestly, and without self-
consciousness.

He helped her into her coat. 'It's cold, windless and
frosty,' he said. 'It won't disarrange that attractive hair-
do.'

Lorna laughed. 'You're obviously a man who under-
stands women! The wind blowing through one's hair

when going for a walk, is fine, but *not* on the way out to dinner!'

'Yours looks as though you can comb it through at any time . . . natural,' he added. 'Under the light it's like autumn leaves.'

'Flatterer . . . never trust a man who flatters you!'

He laughed and retorted, 'I don't particularly want to be trusted!'

They went out into the November air which was filled with the earthy smell of damp vegetation, dying bonfires and chrysanthemums. A full moon rode through layers of cloud without being able to illuminate the scene for more than a few seconds at a time, and their footsteps echoed eerily in the deep silence. Guy put a hand on her elbow and saw her into his car, peering at her and smiling. There was no strangeness.

A few minutes later they drove past Felicity's house. Lorna wondered if he would mention her.

He said easily, 'I expect Felicity has told you we are old friends.'

'Yes.' Lorna turned towards him in the darkness.

'I didn't want to go into details that night at the hospital.' He paused and then added, 'I expect she also told you that I'm going to be her doctor from now on. And look after her mother when she returns, should she need me.'

Lorna exclaimed, 'No, no, she didn't mention that.' Her surprise bordered on shock. It had seemed almost automatic that Matthew would take over the role.

Guy sounded baffled as he said, 'I should have thought Matthew would have explained, since you work with him all the time.' He hastened, not wishing to give the matter too much importance, 'I expect it slipped his

mind . . . doctors remember everything and nothing—
we're an odd crowd.'

Lorna was left with the strange feeling that, while she
had been told facts, some vital truth had been omitted.
Was it that Matthew did not want to accept as a patient
someone with whom he was emotionally involved?

They reached Malmesbury a short while later. It was a
town where history was sanctified in stone and sculpture,
both Saxon and Norman glorifying in the magnificent
remains of the Abbey. The Apostle Spoon was by the
Market Cross which dated from the reign of Henry VII.
Nearby stood the fourteenth-century clock tower of the
parish church, opposite which a large mirror warned of
oncoming traffic. The moon found a space in the clouds
and flooded the scene with golden light as Guy parked
his car practically outside the restaurant. The silence
seemed to throb with the echoes of the past, bringing
yesterday nearer, and making today seem unreal.

'If only one could live through the different ages,'
Lorna said dreamily as she stood, listening, and gazing
around her at the quaint buildings and antiquity of it
all.

Guy laughed. 'It takes me all my time to live in the
twentieth century!'

Lorna wondered if Matthew would have understood
what she meant and felt.

The Apostle Spoon offered sanctuary in its candle-lit
dining-room. It was small, beamed, and 'the oldest
house in the oldest borough in England', as it described
itself.

Guy was known there, and after having drinks in the
bar downstairs they settled at their window table and
Lorna was able to assess him for the first time. A man,

she guessed, who lived life to the full, and who would not take kindly to gloom or depression.

'What are your plans for the future?' he asked suddenly and directly when, after a simple meal of smoked salmon and fillet steak, they reached the coffee stage.

'I've only just joined Matthew,' she replied, somewhat amazed.

'You're not cut out merely to be an assistant,' he countered.

'We all have to start.'

'Exactly. I want to know where you intend to *go*. Matthew will never take a partner.'

'No one can speak for his, or her, future, let alone someone else's,' she said challengingly.

'*Touché!* But I know Matthew.'

'You *think* you know him.'

'Do you?' He sipped his coffee. 'I mean, do you *imagine you* know him?'

Lorna lowered her gaze and then raised it disarmingly, 'I'm not given to flights of fancy,' she said.

He laughed and smoothed his tie with a little confident gesture. 'Which means that in reality you would like to become his partner,' came the cool confident retort.

Lorna faced the fact that Guy was right, although she had not previously admitted it to herself. 'Very well . . . yes, I *would* like that.'

Guy leaned back in his chair, one arm stretched out towards his coffee cup, and looked at her very steadily. 'I need a woman in my practice,' he said with an air of conviction. 'A partner. You can join me any time you like.' He added with a smile, 'And before you begin to get all indignant because you think I'm going behind

Matthew's back to steal his assistant, I've already told him my intentions.'

Lorna stared at him, incredulous.

'What did he say?' Her heart was racing; a sudden apprehension overwhelmed her.

'His exact words were, "Fair enough. So long as I know".'

'Oh.' Lorna's voice was a trifle breathless and flat.

'But,' Guy added, 'I don't know, or can't make out, whether that remark was indicative of acceptance, or a challenge. Be that as it may, I've made the offer. Consider it.'

Lorna thought that she had come out to dinner to enjoy herself, and relax, and was now thrown into confusion and conflict. A partnership in Guy Hadwell's firm. Just like that! And why hadn't Matthew told her? He had not shown the slightest interest in her going out with Guy. He was, she thought furiously, the most impossible man and her first impressions of him were correct, when she told herself that she could not tolerate working with him! '*Fair enough*', indeed! It would serve him right if she were to leave him in the lurch . . . except that they had the statutory six months' agreement!

There was a quiet confidence about Guy as he observed her, which was unnerving. This was a situation new to her. Not the pleasant, mildly flirtatious dinner, with sensual overtones and the prospect of an intimate relationship eventually to follow.

'There's one other thing,' he said, and now he leaned forward and held his brandy glass in both hands, 'I fell in love with you at first sight that night at the hospital . . . and I want to marry you, Lorna.' He hurried on, 'And if you tell me that this is ridiculous, and all the rest of the platitudes, then I'll bore you to death by quoting the poets to prove that there is nothing unusual in it all. I didn't merely ask you out to dinner to talk small talk, or be flirtatious. I don't expect response, but at least you will know the situation and not be deceived by anything I may do, or say!' He stopped, aware of her utter amazement. 'And that was quite a speech,' he added.

'"Speech",' she echoed. 'It was the scenario of a television play!'

He made a wry face. 'Surely not as bad as *that*,' he quipped, and then looked solemn. 'I'm serious,' he insisted. 'Don't look so shattered.'

'But you don't *know* me,' Lorna insisted. 'I'm a stranger.'

'My father saw my mother in a florist's shop,' he said, 'and decided there and then, that he wanted to marry her. They were married six weeks later and now, after thirty-five years, they're *still* married and still in love. I must have inherited the virus! I shan't change.' There was a ring of confidence in his voice.

Lorna's words came jerkily, 'You—you didn't tell Matthew this?'

'Good heavens, no! Matthew hasn't any time for emotion.' Guy seemed about to enlarge on the remark, and then gave a little enigmatic smile. 'Matthew regards me as a gregarious, flirtatious lover of the ladies! True in its way, I suppose. This is quite different,' he finished solemnly.

Lorna couldn't either ridicule, or be annoyed, by his protestations. She knew instinctively and somewhat shatteringly, that he was sincere. She looked at him almost critically, assessing his value as a prospective husband. He was certainly good-looking, with laughter lines around his eyes and a mobile humorous mouth. No secrets here; no hidden depths. She felt that she knew more about him after an hour or two than she knew about Matthew after weeks. In fact, she argued, she knew nothing whatsoever about Matthew. The fact gave Guy the advantage. She liked him, but that was vastly different from loving him. The idea of his wanting to marry her was absurd. *Love at first sight.* Of course it was a possibility and recognised by the romantics, but somehow one only expected to *read* about it rather than encounter it.

'There's nothing I can say to you,' Lorna murmured. 'I can't imagine your being—'

'Don't say "a friend",' he cut in.

'If I'm to see you again, then it is certainly just a question of friendship,' she insisted.

He studied her intently. 'Suppose we don't plan for tomorrow,' he suggested, and looked thoughtful. 'Friends.' A smile hovered on his lips. 'Very well. You know how I feel and I shall not give up unless you marry someone else. Is that plain?'

'Quite.'

'Are you likely to marry someone else?' He shot the question at her.

She shook her head. 'No, I've no desire to marry anyone at the moment, I assure you.'

'Then it's up to me to make you change your mind,' he said forcefully. 'We'll leave it at that. I shan't become a nuisance I promise you.'

She looked at him and said with honesty, 'I like you, Guy. And I've enjoyed this evening, even if it has been somewhat unusual.'

'Good . . . and there are no strings to the partnership

offer. Marriage is not part of the deal.' He finished his brandy. 'I don't mind having a professional partner as well as a wife, or the one without the other. Your options are open.' His smile broadened. 'This has been a splendid evening. Where would you like to go next time?'

Lorna laughed. 'Give me strength to get over this evening!'

He put his hand across the table and touched hers.

'I love you,' he said gently. 'Remember that.'

Lorna remembered those words when she saw Matthew the following Monday morning. Would he ask about the evening? And had he spent part of Sunday with Felicity?

As was often the case, he might have read her thoughts, because he said, 'Well? Did you enjoy the Apostle Spoon?'

'Very much.' She met his inscrutable gaze. 'You know already that Guy intended asking me to join him.'

'Yes, how do you feel about it, later on?' He was standing at his desk, turning over the letters Mrs Keen had placed there, and he looked up, surveying her with interest.

'I'll tell you when my six months here are up.' She raised her head. 'Obviously I don't want to remain an assistant. I didn't qualify just for that.'

'Naturally. You'll have to see. Guy's a good chap and you can rely on his word. He also has a very good practice which will expand.'

'He should employ you as his publicity agent,' Lorna's voice had an edge to it.

'Doctors are not allowed to advertise,' he reminded

her with infuriating calm . . . 'Oh, before I forget, Felicity invited us both for drinks tomorrow evening.'

'"Us both"?' Lorna echoed, surprised.

'Yes . . . If you'd rather not—'

'On the contrary, I'd like it.' Lorna was intrigued.

'Good; we'll go about seven. Her mother is returning on December 12th, by the way. Which reminds me, I've not had the pleasure of meeting your parents.'

'They haven't been able to get away, but they're coming for Christmas . . . How did Clare's case go off yesterday? No complications?'

'None. She'll be out tomorrow.' He sighed as though he had a problem on his hands. 'It's a question of how she adjusts and whether she will have learned from experience.'

'If we learned from experience,' Lorna said quietly, 'doctors' consulting rooms would be half-empty.'

'Ah!' It was a sound of agreement.

Lorna held Matthew's gaze as she said, 'Guy told me that he is going to look after Felicity and her mother professionally.'

Matthew appeared to be concentrating on his desk. 'Yes,' he agreed briefly. 'Would you ask Mrs Keen to come in; I must get through some of these reports.'

Lorna had the feeling that Matthew was watching her as she walked to the door and hurried away. His inscrutability infuriated her.

Guy telephoned her just as she was about to telephone him to thank him for 'a most enjoyable evening'.

He said eagerly, 'I understand you are going to Cornerways . . . So am I. We can hardly slip away and have dinner somewhere . . . but I'd like to arrange for you to come to see where I live.'

'Willow Lodge,' Lorna said knowledgeably. She added swiftly, 'I must go. A patient.'

'Talk to you tomorrow,' he murmured.

Lorna replaced the receiver with a little smile of satisfaction.

When Matthew and Lorna were ready to drive over to Cornerways the following evening (Lorna having remained at Gable's End to see a patient), the telephone rang just as they were about to leave the house. Matthew groaned and picked up the receiver of the instrument in the hall, his voice slightly clipped, then, 'Felicity! We're just coming over . . . your *mother*! At Heathrow! But I thought you said the 12th Dec . . . Oh, not too well.' He repeated the conversation for Lorna's benefit. 'Of course we understand . . . But I don't like the idea of your driving there to fetch her—not alone. I'm not being silly and don't argue.' He listened patiently for a few seconds, and then exclaimed with finality, 'All the same, I'm coming with you. It's about a hundred miles from here to London; less, of course, to Heathrow. I'll be over right away and we'll go in my car—it's bigger.' He laughed. 'And for heaven's sake put on some warm clothes. It isn't summer. I'm not being dictatorial. You need looking after . . . see you in a few minutes.'

The receiver went back with a decisive click. 'You got the gist of all that,' he said to Lorna.

Lorna stood there, deflated. She had been looking forward to the evening with anticipation and a degree of curiosity. Now Matthew was going to Heathrow with Felicity, and Heathrow seemed like another continent.

'How about Guy?' she asked suddenly, and on a note of hope.

'He had to cry off, anyway. A midder.' Matthew

darted into the adjoining cloakroom and snatched a scarf and overcoat, mumbling, 'May be glad of these.'

'I should think so,' Lorna said stoutly. 'It is *you* who breeze around half the time as though it were summer!'

It dawned on Matthew that Lorna's evening had been spoilt and that he had taken it for granted that she would remain on duty.

'I'm sorry about all this,' he said apologetically. 'Do you mind holding the fort? Transfer the calls to your number and I'll contact the exchange when I get back. I should think around midnight.' He added, 'And would you tell Mrs Cummings our change of plans. She'll be in her sitting room watching television.'

He opened the front door and an icy gust of wind blew in. Lorna stood in the shaft of light from the hall. A lamp near the porch—identifying the house at all times— threw a glow over Matthew's car as it stood in the drive.

'Get in out of the cold,' he called as he slid into the driving seat. ''Bye.' The engine revved up and he shot off as though on a race track.

Lorna returned to her cottage which seemed bleak and empty.

CHAPTER FOUR

LORNA met Felicity's mother, Grace Anson, a week later when she, Lorna, Matthew and Guy were invited to Cornerways for drinks—to make up for the evening that had to be cancelled.

As Lorna drove there, she felt that she was being unwittingly drawn into a circle against her will and instincts. The fact that she liked Felicity had nothing to do with it, she argued, wanting only the calm and peace of remaining on the periphery of Matthew's social life. She shrank from conflict, while knowing that she and Matthew engendered it. Nevertheless the prospect of seeing Guy again brought a bubble of happiness, particularly as their meeting at Willow Lodge had not materialised owing to minor crises in his practice. Her interest was sharpened by curiosity. His offer of both a professional partnership, and one of marriage, struck an original and tempting note.

Grace Anson was nothing she had expected, having visualised her as a rather overpowering, independent type, accustomed to having her own way. Actually she was small, slim and frail, with a fine, taut skin and china-blue eyes, friendly and warm, even if faintly clouded by sadness. Since Lorna understood that Grace had been widowed a matter of a few years previously, the explanation sufficed.

'I'm Grace,' she said in greeting, 'and so happy to meet you. I know how very kind you have been to

Felicity . . . Matthew not with you?'

'Doing a visit *en route*,' Lorna explained, aware that Matthew had already been over to Cornerways on at least two occasions during the past week and was therefore well acquainted.

'Oh, splendid. One never knows with doctors, and I upset things last time.'

'Are you feeling better?' Lorna eyed her with professional scrutiny.

Grace waved a hand in dismissal. 'It was nothing—jet lag,' she lied. 'I've decided my roving days are over, and now that Felicity has settled here . . .'

The words were significant and Lorna asked, 'You mean that you will—' She broke off, realising that she was being intrusive.

'I shall stay here—with her,' came the confident reply. 'We've seen too little of each other since her father died, and she needs someone to run the house. Domesticity has never been her forte!'

Lorna forced a smile. 'It isn't mine, either. Necessity drives one!'

'And you have so *much* responsibility,' came the sincere comment. 'I'm full of admiration.'

'Thank you,' Lorna laughed. 'Doctors are two a penny these days, you know.'

The door bell rang—a sustained ring.

'That's Matthew,' Felicity cried, appearing at the top of the staircase. 'It's an impatient ring. Guy's is shorter and not so loud!' She hurried and greeted Matthew with a bright, 'Hello!'

He came in, Lorna thought, with a purposeful air as though in command of the house, but when speaking to Grace he became slightly subdued, his eyes searching

her face with faint anxiety. It was obvious they had
already established an easy familiarity, built, no doubt,
Lorna thought, on his already solid relationship with
Felicity.

'Feeling rested?' he asked.

'Yes.' She had a gentle musical voice and, in repose,
looked beautiful. Felicity was not in the least like her
and gave the impression of being quite happy to let
Grace take command. At that moment Felicity had a
far-away expression in her eyes, absent-mindedly looking around her and then, suddenly alert, cried, 'That's
Guy!'

Guy joined them, relaxed, pleasant but, Lorna felt,
watchful, as he looked from face to face reflectively; his
gaze lingering imperceptibly on Matthew without
apparent reason. Was he trying to sum up Matthew's
feelings for Felicity?

I love you, Lorna. His words echoed and, almost as
though by telepathy, he met Lorna's gaze—a gaze which
Matthew intercepted before turning his attention to
Grace.

Lorna felt almost embarrassed, aware of Matthew to
the point where her heart missed a beat since his attitude
appeared to be one of disapproval. Or was she indulging
in fantasy? She moved a distance away from him and
gave her attentions to Guy, finding it difficult to assess
his attitude to Felicity, or hers to him, while remembering Felicity's words at the cottage, '*I had a lover from
whom I parted amicably*'. Was Guy that lover? And why
build up fanciful pictures out of ghosts in order to give
the past importance when it was, after all, no concern of
hers? Lorna asked herself impatiently.

They drank their respective drinks and ate the

canapés at which Mrs Nilson excelled, talking, laughing, yet in an atmosphere of vigilance as though each had a reservation about the other when it came to exchanging confidences. Only Lorna was free from what appeared to be inhibitions, and she noticed that Guy's easy manner was somewhat restricted, although he did his best to conceal it by banter and wit. Matthew several times lapsed into silence, but it would have been difficult to associate his attitude with boredom. Lorna had a curious feeling that he found it impossible to adapt to several people in a group, being at his best with one.

There was no apparent reason why Grace's presence should have been restrictive, for she was ebullient and full of anecdotes about her trips to California and Hong Kong. And then, as she got to her feet, she swayed dizzily, put her hand out gropingly towards the arm of her chair and dropped into it, murmuring, 'It's nothing . . . I just feel faint sometimes.' She gave Matthew and Guy a warning look, 'And I don't want any fuss . . . too hot in here, probably.' She turned to Lorna. 'Just a glass of water,' she said weakly, the colour having drained from her face, leaving her pallid and drawn. A minute or two later she said insistently, 'I'm quite all right now . . . and I don't need doctors! Since there are three of you here!'

'That will be for me to decide,' Guy exclaimed with authority.

Grace waved an arm, forced a little laugh and suggested, 'Why don't the four of you go off to dinner somewhere—' She stopped, faintly embarrassed because she realised she was assuming control and making suggestions which might be reasonable for Guy and Felicity, but not for Matthew and Lorna.

Felicity hastened, 'I certainly should not leave you this evening . . . but we could easily have something here.' She conveyed the impression that she was eager for them to remain together far longer than merely for drinks.

Guy hedged; he had hoped to take Lorna out. Matthew's expression held uncertainty. But Lorna spoke up, 'That would be lovely—provided I can help raid the 'fridge with you.'

Felicity brightened. 'Oh, good.' She looked appealingly at Matthew and Guy.

They capitulated, faintly wary of each other.

The meal was eaten picnic-fashion, and made up of many delectable dishes which Felicity had purchased 'in case of' from a famous store. Grace, Lorna noticed, made a valiant attempt at finishing her particular choice and Lorna knew that she was feeling far from well. Conversation flowed and they all caught the spark of enthusiasm which builds up from good food and wine, relaxing as laughter took the place of reserve; but when the time came to leave, Lorna made a hurried escape before either Matthew or Guy had a chance to waylay her.

She had not been home more than a few minutes when the door bell rang and, to her amazement, Matthew stood there.

'I wondered if I might be offered a thimble-full of brandy,' he said with a wry smile.

She mastered her surprise and said in friendly tone, 'By all means . . . come in.'

'You left so hurriedly,' he complained, as they walked into the sitting room. 'It *did* occur to me that you and Guy might have had a previous engagement, in which case I could soon have made myself scarce.'

Lorna shook her head, indicated the drinks tray, and said, 'All yours.'

He poured two small brandies, seated himself in an armchair opposite her, stretched out his legs and said, 'This is perfect . . . We may fight, clash in many ways, but you can be a very restful person.'

'Sounds about as thrilling as a rice pudding,' she said. Nevertheless she was amazed by the assessment; it was the nearest he had come to expressing any opinion about their relationship. He was, she thought, an incredible man. His presence constituted a challenge no matter what the circumstances. The conflict might lie just beneath the surface, but at the moment he appealed to every human instinct. The contradiction was, in itself, an attraction.

He laughed, surveyed her, and said unexpectedly, 'I didn't mean it that way.'

The telephone broke shrilly into the momentary silence.

Matthew groaned; Lorna answered it, feeling impatient.

'Guy!' Her surprise was obvious.

'Why did you vanish like that?'

'It was far too cold to stand about,' she said on a note of laughter.

'Are you free tomorrow evening?'

'Yes, I think so.'

'Come and have a meal with me here. I want you to see Willow Lodge.'

'I'd enjoy that,' she agreed, and while Matthew was not watching her, his presence was intrusive.

'About seven. I suppose you'd better come in your car

in case of emergencies, otherwise I'd pick you up and see
you safely home.'

'It's a considerate thought, but I'll come on my own.
Less complicated.'

'Very well . . . it's too late to get together now, I
suppose?' There was a hopeful note in his voice.

Lorna didn't mention Matthew, merely said, 'Far too
late . . . tomorrow, then.'

He said reluctantly, 'Yes . . . good night, Lorna.'

She replaced the receiver and returned to her chair.
Matthew's expression was devoid of curiosity, or apparent interest, although he obviously knew from
whom the call came.

'I'm not happy about Grace,' he said with concern. He
might have known her for years instead of a week.

'Probably the strain, excitement, and general upheaval. You know, of course, that she is going permanently to live with Felicity. She told me this evening,
before you arrived.'

Matthew nodded. 'It has been discussed. I don't
usually subscribe to parents and children sharing a
house, but the circumstances seem to point to the
arrangement being beneficial in their case. Felicity has a
great deal of work to get through, and Grace will be a
tremendous help to her . . . don't you agree?'

Lorna felt slightly irritated. She wasn't in the mood to
discuss the Ansons.

'I agree with people doing precisely what suits
them. When it comes to it, they will eventually do
as they please, irrespective of anything that may be
said.'

'On the principle that no one takes advice,' he said, his
voice sharp.

'Since people often don't even listen to what the doctor says—yes. We ask for guidance and then go off and do precisely as we intended in the first place!' She felt on edge, disliking the change of mood. 'But, then, you may have particular influence over Felicity.'

'You contradict yourself,' he suggested, as though scoring a point.

'Exceptions to every rule.' She had wondered if he would talk about himself, progress from his opening remarks which touched the fringe of intimacy.

'You evidently are not in sympathy with the arrangement.' It was a flat statement.

'It may not seem so ideal when Felicity wants to marry. It is easier to set up house than to change the pattern, should it be necessary.' Was it his protective instinct towards Felicity that made the arrangement appeal to him?

A flicker of resistance went over his face as he said, 'Since she hasn't any plans to marry at the moment, that problem can wait.' He added, 'You *talk* of living for today, but I notice you always allow for the eventualities of tomorrow.'

'While you,' she countered, temper rising, 'completely ignore the past which, so far as you are concerned, is an absolute mystery . . . That makes us even.'

There was a silence so heavy that it seemed to take all the oxygen from the room. For a second anger blazed in his eyes, and his lips tightened; then an expression of haunting sadness clouded his features as he said in a low, controlled voice, 'One day I'll satisfy your curiosity, Lorna—but only at the right time and place.'

Lorna was trembling, ashamed of her outburst, finding it unaccountable and inexcusable; but there was something about him that goaded her, brought out the worst in her nature.

He put his brandy glass down on the table with deliberate precision.

'Thank you,' he said politely as he got to his feet.'No, don't get up—I'll see myself out.' There was an air of weary sadness about him as he heaved himself into his overcoat and threw his scarf round his neck, moving to the door as he did so.

Lorna sat there, seemingly paralysed.

'Good night,' he murmured quietly, and was gone.

The cottage might have been emptied of furniture; the fire raked out; the heating turned off. Only the sound of the wind whining and moaning broke the terrible silence. It would have been so much easier had he gone out in a rage, so that she could have countered with matching wrath. As it was she faced the unbearable humiliation of self-disgust. Tears stung her eyes as regret struck at the pit of her stomach, making her feel sick. She knew, also, that an apology would merely add insult to injury.

There was nothing in Matthew's manner the following morning to indicate that the episode had ever taken place.

It was Mrs Keen who said, 'Doctor's tired. The Lacy baby arrived, but, of course, you know. Glad it's a girl; they've three boys and this was a last gamble.' She eyed Lorna intently, 'Are you all right?'

'*The Lacy baby arrived*'. A simple fact, except that, normally, Matthew would have mentioned it since they had been involved, and she had said she would like to be present at the birth. There were some patients who, while not friends, were nevertheless 'special'. Jim and Jean Lacy were among them, and Matthew had delivered two of the boys.

Lorna braced herself and met Mrs Keen's perceptive gaze.

'I think the wind had a bad effect on me,' she managed to say with a laugh. 'It howled around my cottage and kept me awake half the night. I hate it . . . Now the Lacys will be able to relax, and spoil the new baby atrociously. A lovely family.'

'We need more like them,' Mrs Keen agreed. 'Oh, Mrs Simms is your first appointment this morning,' she added significantly.

Mrs Simms was one of those cases that baffled doctors and surgeons alike. She had been married for ten years, longed for children, but had never conceived. Periodically, she would come back to be 'seen', asking if there was something more that could be done. Lorna, as a comparative 'new' doctor, offered hope—quite erroneously—because Lorna could only listen, and reiterate all the facts.

'But Mrs Simms,' she said gently, 'both you and your husband have been thoroughly checked. There's no blockage between the sperm and the egg—'

'When I had that anaesthetic,' Mrs Simms cut in, 'something about a dye and a lapa—' She sighed. 'I'm no good at remembering medical terms.'

'A blue dye was injected through the cervix to make sure that the way was clear—a laparoscope was inserted in your tummy to watch the dye's progress and check that the fallopian tubes could catch the eggs released by the ovary, and that there were no adhesions outside the tubes to kink it.'

Moira Simms nodded; there were tears in her eyes. She was thirty, an attractive woman, with an excellent figure and well-groomed appearance. Now she looked weak and pathetic.

'When you came here, I thought that you might suggest something—work a miracle. Some new idea . . . I feel a freak—'

'Now that is ridiculous,' Lorna said sharply. 'You are a healthy, normal and attractive woman—'

'What is the good of all that if I can't conceive?'

Lorna could not tell her that although her condition defied all medical precepts, it was more than possible that, should she take a lover, or even a new husband, she might well conceive without trouble. And that was no reflection on the virility of her present husband, who was equally normal with a high and active sperm count.

'I *wish* I could help,' Lorna said earnestly. 'If you could forget about it—'

'I never forget about it.'

'That's self-defeating. Look at the number of people who adopt a child, and then have one of their own after years of trying to do so.'

'Then it's indirectly my fault,' came the despairing wail.

'A question of *fault* doesn't come into it,' Lorna persisted, thinking how sad it was that such a young and healthy woman should be so unhappy.

'It's—it's ruining our sex life.' The words rushed out.

'Anxiety is a poor substitute for enthusiasm,' Lorna commented. 'Besides, your husband—'

'He's getting tired of it,' Moira Simms burst out. 'I'm beginning to irritate him.' She sighed and finished almost bitterly, 'He has reconciled himself to the situation.' It was an overt criticism. 'I've suggested going away for Christmas, but—'

The reminder of Christmas struck a chill at Lorna's heart. She didn't feel like Christmas with all its festivities and parties. Depression seeped into her.

'A good idea,' she agreed.

'Jim says, what's the good of our having a holiday if I'm going to take the problem away with us, and ruin everything? He hasn't any *sympathy*.' Her voice was choked.

Lorna looked at her very steadily. 'Would you rather have a child, or your husband?' she asked quietly.

Moira Simms started, wide-eyed, almost accusing.

'It isn't a *question* of that,' she replied, her voice rising.

'But it could be,' Lorna warned her, 'if you continue as you are. Obviously your husband loves you enough to adjust to life without children, and to make the best of the situation. You, on the other hand, seem unable even to contemplate being reconciled. My question still stands.'

'But—' There was a sudden change of expression, 'I couldn't—couldn't think of life without Jim. I love him—'

'Then love him enough to put him first,' Lorna suggested boldly. 'Who knows, by doing that you may even get the child you want so desperately. If he can accept the disappointment, isn't it only fair that you, too, should follow his example? He probably thinks that, no matter what the tests may prove, you blame *him*.'

There was a great stillness in the room, and it was several seconds before Moira Simms spoke. When she did her voice was broken, but held a new strength.

'You are right. Of course you are right. I've contributed nothing constructive to the problem. Nothing,' she added. 'I've only thought of myself.'

'Then stop being selfish, and who knows what may happen?'

Moira Simms bowed her head, chastened.

'Thank you,' she whispered. 'Oh, *thank* you. I needed to face up to the truth.'

Matthew saw Moira Simms walking down the corridor to the front door.

'Mrs Simms looks brighter,' he said to Lorna a little later. 'Is she pregnant?'

Lorna shook her head. 'Just a question of priorities,' she answered simply.

'Ah.' His voice was deep. 'Very few of us get those right.'

They looked at each other, and in that moment there seemed to be a silent truce and a renewal of good faith. Lorna's spirits lifted.

'Have you any plans for Christmas?' he asked irrelevantly. 'I remember your parents are coming down.'

'I've nothing arranged, and my parents are not coming until Boxing Day. Some special function changed their plans.' She met his gaze. 'Why?'

'Because I wondered if you'd care to join me on Christmas Day,' he said unexpectedly. 'I know it's a few weeks away, but I'd like to get in first.'

There was a conciliatory attitude about him, as though he had come to terms with a problem and wished to create the right atmosphere. The last thing she had expected.

'That would be fun.' There was no hesitation in her acceptance.

'I shall invite Felicity and Grace,' he said firmly. 'They don't know anyone here, and the more the merrier, to use a cliché. Mrs Cummings feels cheated if she doesn't have a celebration once a year.' He sighed regretfully. 'Celebrations are not really in my line, but Christmas—' His eyes brightened and then clouded. 'Anyway, that's settled. Guy will look in for a drink sometime,' he added.

Lorna could imagine Guy having a series of parties, his house probably full of guests, or relatives. She knew that he had a brother and sister, and his parents lived in Bredon about thirty-six miles away.

Matthew held her gaze with sudden intensity. 'How about having dinner with me on Christmas Eve? Get into the spirit of it all. I know just the right place, very near here. We can talk and fight as the mood dictates,' he added whimsically.

Lorna gave a little chuckle, feeling pleased, 'Very well,' she agreed.

'And I'll concentrate on the talk angle,' he promised, a significant note in his voice which gave the words importance.

'I'll hold you to that,' she warned him, their eyes meeting again, their gaze holding and then falling away.

The following weeks slipped by, the trees stark against the sky. Mists gathered in the valleys, and blurred the outline of hills and distant fields. Lights began to twinkle in shop windows, and Christmas trees appeared in holly-decorated rooms; while mistletoe hung in tantalising places, tempting and flirtatious. There were the usual grumbles and groans, the laughter of children, the anticipation of lovers; the warm eagerness of parents awaiting the arrival of 'the family'. Every town and village had an expectant air, tinsel flashed amid cotton-wool snow; the door bells in village stores hardly stopped tinkling as customers packed in, smiles lurking behind the harassment.

Lorna saw Guy on several occasions before Christmas Eve.

'How about New Year?' he said gaily. 'Can't do anything about Christmas, I'm afraid; although you could come to Bredon with me on Boxing Day. I'd love you to meet my parents. You'd like them, and they you.'

Meeting his parents seemed a momentous step. Lorna didn't want to be accepted as having any definite place in his life; neither did she want to lose the pleasure of his friendship.

'I'm spending Christmas Day with Matthew.'

Guy said, a trifle shortly, 'Are you now . . . The Ansons, as well?'

Lorna shot him a look of surprise. 'Yes. Why do you ask?'

He looked a little awkward. 'Curiosity. They've struck up a good friendship.'

A thought struck Lorna. 'Didn't you agree with their coming to Tetbury?'

'I'd no idea Felicity *was* coming here,' he replied. 'You know that.'

Lorna apologised. 'Of course; how silly of me.' It occurred to her that whenever the Anson name was mentioned it appeared to create tension.

'New Year's Eve?' he persisted, his gaze earnest.

'A lot can happen between now and then,' she suggested surprisingly.

'Meaning that you don't want to commit yourself?'

She shook her head. 'No, I'd like to join you.'

He smiled broadly. 'Then that's settled. I usually have open house,' he warned her. 'Would you mind?'

'Of course not.'

'I want you to meet my friends . . . you're an elusive creature,' he added, and his attitude was partly complimentary and partly regretful.

Lorna laughed, but didn't contradict him.

Christmas Eve was a crisp, sunlit day with frost lying white over the countryside like a carpet of snow. In late afternoon a technicolour sunset rifted the blue sky, forming crimson rivers that cut between mountains of cloud, whose peaks rose fiery and awesome as rainbow colours, smudged with grey, dyed the scene. Reflected light spread over landscape and houses, pouring molten gold upon windows, turning them into mysterious worlds set in shimmering opal-tinted dusk. And as the moon eventually gained supremacy, the glow changed and a serene silver radiance lay upon the land.

Matthew and Lorna looked at each other as he collected her at the cottage at seven.

'A perfect night,' they said in unison. Around them the quaint, lop-sided cottages nestled in the shadows, as though aware of the hectic last-minute activities going on within their walls.

'I feel guilty because I'm not doing anything by way of preparation for tomorrow,' Lorna said, the guilt increasing as she faced the fact that she was glad her parents were not coming until Boxing Day—for which she was already prepared.

Matthew drove the short distance to The Wayfarer

near Tetbury, where he was well-known—the owners being patients. They had reserved him a secluded table set in an alcove where he and Lorna could talk without being overheard, or disturbed in any way. A great log-fire burned in a vast chimney-corner, and refectory tables with dazzlingly white napery and cut-glass completed the picture of elegance and comfort. The decor was a blend of old and new, and sapphire velvet cushions adorned the monks' benches, the velvet duplicated at the windows.

'It's a quiet night,' the proprietor—a cheerful welcoming man who had spent many years in Italy—said almost approvingly, knowing the rush that lay ahead, with a special Christmas celebration, to say nothing of New Year.

'This restaurant relies on recommendation,' Matthew explained to Lorna, 'and has the supreme advantage of being on our doorstep.'

It was, Lorna thought, typical that he had never mentioned it before. Just then she noticed the champagne in the ice bucket beside their table and a wave of excitement surged over her. This was her first outing with him, and it was interesting to see him as a host. His smooth easy manner, friendliness to the staff and air of authority, created just the right atmosphere.

He drew her gaze to his. 'Have you summed me up to your satisfaction?' he demanded, his voice startling in its challenge.

'No,' she replied honestly, 'and I doubt if I ever shall.'

The wine waiter paused beside the champagne.

'Pour it,' Matthew said with a smile.

A few seconds later he raised his glass and looked at

her intently. 'To the first of many,' he said as suspense mounted.

Lorna was conscious, as always, of the tension that seemed to build up around him. Everything he said had an element of the unexpected about it. The scene they were now enacting seemed out of character for him. A perfect restaurant, soft lights, all the elements that constituted romance. Yet she had not accompanied him dreaming, or even thinking, of any romantic, or flirtatious, occasion. Perhaps that was his greatest attraction: the man who would never attempt to flirt, or to make love. Her pulse quickened as she compared him with Guy . . . Guy wanted to marry her. The possibility lay at the back of her mind, tantalisingly.

The menus had been brought and they studied them.

'I know,' she said, half-apologetically, 'that I shall be having turkey tomorrow, but I fancy it now. Do you mind?'

He gave a little chuckle. 'Why should I? I've not had any for a year, so I'll join you. Have our own particular Christmas to celebrate the fact that we've not yet come to blows! And to begin with?'

'Avocado and prawns,' she said without hesitation.

They closed the large artistically-designed menus.

The cloying romantic nonsense which causes so much upheaval in marriage.

The echo of those words seemed suddenly to throb in the momentary silence and Lorna felt shattered by them. How could one really have a relationship of any depth with a man who held such sentiments? The spark which had lit a previous enthusiasm died, she felt empty and deflated, but managed to say provocatively as she sipped her champagne, 'I'm quite sure that there have been times when you wanted to fight with me, Matthew.'

'The desire being mutual,' he replied. 'But, on the whole, it has been quite a peaceful and friendly association.' He looked at her inquiringly.

'Yes.' She spoke tentatively.

'For which I'm very grateful, believe me,' he said sincerely. 'I had an assistant some time ago, who wanted continual praise, adulation and flirtation—not necessarily in that order. Nearly drove me mad!' His voice rose, his expression sufficiently appalled to be amusing.

Lorna could not help saying, 'You're a strange man. I sometimes wonder if you have any normal emotions whatsoever!'

She waited for the explosion that didn't come. Instead, he said in an almost devastatingly harsh voice, 'All I ask is peace—not conflict; and serious emotion means conflict. You accused me of being a mystery, Lorna—' He paused and looked down into his glass, his silence tense and heavy with suspense.

'I ought never to have said that,' she said. 'It was—'

'Perfectly natural in the circumstances,' he countered generously. 'Everything must seem a mystery to you, but we are apt to draw away from the truths that hurt us . . . you see, I haven't a very good background when it comes to appraising marriage, love, emotion . . . When I was six, my mother left my father for another man, smashing up what had been considered an ideally happy marriage.'

Lorna gave a little cry of sorrow and dismay.

'My father idolised her, and never got over it.' A passionate sadness darkened his eyes as he added painfully, 'He committed suicide when I was eight.'

Lorna heard the words with a sickening awareness of

suffering. Her voice was husky with sympathy as she said simply, 'Oh, Matthew, I'm so sorry.'

'I said I would tell you at the right time and place.' He looked at her with an earnestness she never forgot. 'Now I feel that you are a *friend*—' the words came revealingly—'who will understand. It may seem strange, but even after all these years, I can still re-live the fear and misery of those two years, when nothing was normal. I don't really remember my mother except as a blurred picture, but I have an impression of gaiety and laughter, with parties and what seemed happiness. A sham,' he added bitterly. 'It isn't something one talks about, and why should people be interested, anyway?' There was not so much cynicism in the remark as a dull inevitability.

'And what happened to you?' Lorna's eyes were misted with sympathy.

'I went to live in Sherborne, with an uncle—my father's brother. I was educated at Sherborne,' he went on, 'but that's beside the point. God preserve me from being mawkish. My father had been associated with a Merchant Bank; money was not a problem, and my uncle was a doctor in Sherborne, so I grew up steeped in medicine, and there was never any question of what I wanted to do in life. After I qualified and had a couple of years at the London Hospital, I came here.'

'And your mother?'

'I've never heard anything about her,' he said harshly. 'I loved my father; he was a fine man. Marriage,' he added bitterly, 'the misery and devastation of all the romantic illusions. And I see it every day in this practice. Love is a nine days' wonder, followed by wreckage.'

'Your father—'

He cut in before she could finish. 'Love killed him,' came the ironic retort.

Turbulence and turmoil were stamped on every feature as Matthew sat there, and Lorna felt not only the depth of his suffering, but the distortion which held a shadow of truth.

'There's nothing I can say—' She looked at him long and earnestly. 'Thank you for telling me. I'm sorry I've been so insensitive.'

'You were entitled to my confidence,' he conceded, 'and I realise I must seem a bit of a mystery. But I cannot bring myself to broadcast details. I'm a doctor, not an actor; and I'm not, after all, news!'

'On the contrary,' she said, 'doctors are just as newsworthy as actors. Step out of line and see.'

For the first time a smile touched his lips. 'You're probably right; and now, no more gloom. Telling you has been a great relief. Now, please, the book is closed.'

Lorna nodded.

'There's one question I'd like to ask,' she said after a few seconds of understanding silence.

'And that?' The question was clipped and abrupt.

'Accepting your distrust of marriage, love, and all that goes with it . . . what *is* your idea of marriage, since it can't be ruled out?'

'Friendship and companionship,' he said uncompromisingly. 'Oh, I know I'm regarded as an eligible bachelor,' he went on, without conceit. 'I've come up against match-making mothers in the district who would not be averse to my marrying their daughters.'

Lorna smiled. 'I know that to be true,' she agreed, looking at him with an intent gaze before she said frankly, 'You know, you are a man who ought to have an experimental marriage—one that protects you from emotion and is purely platonic.'

There was a sudden tense silence, during which enthusiasm and interest flashed into his eyes, as he said, 'You're absolutely right. How about joining me in the experiment? Marry me, Lorna.'

CHAPTER FIVE

LORNA heard those words, 'Marry me', as though they were part of a charade, and she stared at him, lips parted, eyes wide and startled.

'Are you serious?' she gasped.

'Just as serious as you were just now, when you suggested I ought to have an experimental platonic marriage to protect me from emotion.' He met her confused gaze with challenge and indomitable strength. 'An experimental marriage,' he repeated with satisfaction. 'Well? It would be ideal for both of us. You don't want ties; neither do I: we're good friends and harmonious colleagues. Precious few marriages have even those advantages.' He smiled broadly—an attractive, half-persuasive smile. 'And if we don't always see eye to eye, then that adds salt to the egg.' He paused for a second and then said, 'Now I want an answer!'

'You demanded that when I was about to join you in the practice,' she reminded him, 'without giving me any time to think.'

'I like action,' he insisted. 'One can argue everything out of existence, losing the substance in the process. And we're unique! Every human being is unique. There is no precedent; the experiment may well have been tried before, but not by *us*. Yes, or no?' His voice remained firm, but there was just a hint of persuasion in it, and his gaze did not leave her face.

But she stood her ground. 'If I say yes,' she warned

him, 'I shouldn't want you to interfere in my life, any more than I should in yours. If we accept this type of marriage, it will have to be one hundred per cent experiment. A marriage of convenience with the bonus of friendship.'

'Agreed.' He sounded both conciliatory and enthusiastic. 'We're taking out an insurance policy against being dragged into all the marriage traumas.' A solemn note crept into his voice as he continued, 'Provided, of course, we do not endanger the reputation of the practice.'

'There is danger in everything,' she reminded him.

'True; but marriage ceremonies these days have become mere interludes on the way to the divorce court!' Bitterness tinged the words. 'You must forgive me for being a realist, but I've an aversion to broken vows, and the sham and hypocrisy of it all . . . When will you marry me?'

'I haven't said I will.' But even as she spoke, Lorna felt almost a compulsion to do so, wanting the security and companionship implicit in the arrangement. No more conflict; no more well-meaning advice: *It's time you were married'*.

'A marriage in name only,' she mused, as though thinking aloud.

He looked composed and relaxed as he said easily, 'Yes; no problems. The house is large enough for us to have our own apartments.' He paused reflectively and then added without trace of embarrassment, 'We can sit over a drink and talk together in the evenings without either having to turn out afterwards, or tongues wagging when we're late.'

'Our friends will be surprised.'

'True friends are never surprised—only interested.'

He added abruptly, 'Are you thinking of Guy?'

'No,' she admitted honestly, 'but now that you've mentioned him . . . I certainly *was* adamant when I told him I'd no intention of marrying in the near future—that was when he offered me a partnership.' She saw no reason why she should mention Guy's proposal. Emotion did not figure in her arrangements with Matthew, therefore confidences were in no way obligatory.

'You will be *my* partner, of course, as well as my wife,' he said, as though taking her acceptance for granted.

A wave of excitement touched her. What mad adventure had she thought up this time?

Silence fell—deep, disturbing. His voice was firm and demanding as he asked in the tone of one who would not repeat the question, 'Will you marry me, Lorna?' His gaze met and held hers.

'Yes,' she replied. 'At least we know precisely where we stand.'

'When?' His voice dropped to a note tinged with appeal, and then hardened as he added, 'I don't want any delay. It would turn an experiment into something laboured and common-place . . . I'll get a special licence and suggest a date immediately after the New Year festivities are over.'

Her voice was a little breathless. 'Early January?'

'Yes, we'll slip away for a few hours and tell everyone afterwards. No use making any exceptions in our confidantes, or the news will travel by Concorde!'

'My parents,' she suggested tentatively.

He smiled at her with understanding. 'We'll make them the exceptions. I'm sure they can be trusted with a secret.'

Lorna nodded. 'A register office: we don't want to

invoke blessings that conflict with our intentions.'

'Well said . . . Would you like your parents to be witnesses? Would they come down?'

Lorna looked delighted. The matter was settled.

'One thing,' Lorna said as an afterthought, 'I take it that we do not explain to anyone that this is no ordinary marriage?'

'No,' he said, and there was a note of austerity in his voice. 'You will be my wife and how we choose to conduct our lives is our own affair . . . Single beds, separate rooms, and all the modern variations,' he added a trifle cynically. 'Mrs Cummings is most intimately associated with our lives. So far as she is concerned, if I chose to sleep on the roof, she would still serve breakfast as usual and tell me what the weather forecast was!' He hastened, 'You'll never cross swords with Mrs Cummings. To begin with, she likes you; secondly, she'll be overjoyed to see me married, and out of the way of those "hussies" as she has, on many occasions, referred to some of my more bizarre patients.' He laughed as he spoke. 'And if you want to entertain your friends, she'll be delighted. Oh, I know she's always regarded me as damned dull. But she has freedom and is well looked after, so she tolerates my defects.'

'You hardly flatter yourself!'

He was silent for a second before saying, 'I suppose I've never been able to *be* myself: if a man doesn't want the emotional turmoil of marriage, then he has to retreat into some kind of protective shell and be very guarded with women.' He beamed at Lorna across the table. 'Now I feel that I've got all A's in my A-levels and am suddenly a free man!'

Lorna absorbed his mood. 'Just when you are about to be *married*!'

'The adventurous experiment! Only you could have thought of it!'

'Which proves how mad I am,' she insisted. 'Heaven knows I hadn't myself in mind when I made the suggestion.'

'All the more intriguing . . . I want a date, Lorna.'

'January 6th,' she said impulsively. 'It's a Friday, and the birthday of a dear friend of mine who happens to be in Switzerland!'

'Thirteen days away,' he said immediately. 'Friday is a good day, too. We can invite a few people over for drinks in the evening and tell them the news, then . . . there's anxiety in your eyes.'

She took a deep breath and said boldly, deciding that it was essential to begin as she meant to keep on, 'I must tell Guy. I can't pretend when avoiding his invitations. I promised to spend New Year's Eve with him.'

Matthew was cool, even placid. 'No reason to change the arrangement.' He sipped his brandy. 'I see your point about telling him. By all means, do. He can certainly be trusted.'

Lorna wanted to mention Felicity, but feared to make her an issue. Obviously, Matthew hadn't felt it necessary to do so. But discretion deserted her as she said almost abruptly, 'How about telling Felicity . . . I mean—'

His expression silenced her as he said somewhat icily, 'My life is far less complicated than yours. Felicity and Grace will thoroughly enjoy the surprise. And, no doubt, be intrigued. Come to think of it, so am I. This is one Christmas Eve we shall *not* forget!'

'Who knows,' she said lightly, 'we might even think it

worthwhile celebrating it in future. Or would nothing cancel your aversion to celebrations—a fact I've noticed with curiosity.'

He drew her gaze to his, held it, and said quietly, but without mawkishness, 'I've never had anything in my life that I've felt worth celebrating. One opts out in a strange kind of way.' Suddenly, unexpectedly, he leaned slightly forward, 'Are you happy, satisfied, about all this? I've no right to take advantage of your original idea just because it was perfect from my point of view.' His voice strengthened, 'My views won't change; neither will my attitude to you.'

Lorna raised her head slightly and her manner was confident, 'That is the point of all this. The whole *experiment*.'

He sighed as he smiled. 'You know, you are an amazing woman.'

'And you are an amazing man,' she said with a significance that was lost on him.

His question was unexpected and abrupt, 'Would you like to select your own wedding ring, or shall I get it, if you tell me your size?'

She didn't hesitate. 'I'd rather you get it; my size is J-and-a-half.'

Almost with precision he took out his diary and wrote the size down in it. Lorna wondered if he had made a note of 'Being married January 6th.'

As if reading her thoughts he said, 'I shan't need reminding of January 6th.' He glanced at his watch and gave an anxious exclamation: 'I promised Robert'—a colleague who was standing in—'I'd be back so that the calls could be transferred by eleven.'

Lorna nodded and a few minutes later they went out

into the winter night. There was a sharp frost and the road looked like a skating rink. She glanced up at him and met his gaze as he was studying her at that exact moment. Between them might have lain the words, *'We're going to be married'*.

On the short drive back, he said, 'What about your cottage?'

She understood the implication and answered, 'I shall keep it for the time being. It might even be useful for the overflow of patients later on.'

'Hedging your bets,' he teased.

'Possibly. I've acted on impulse enough for one evening,' she added with a little laugh.

'Yes, thank God . . . and you may like to entertain your friends there on occasion. It's a charming place, anyway.'

'So is Gable's End . . . we shall have to get a crop of keys cut!'

'Splendid; I always *have* fancied Sunset Cottage,' he laughed, as he drew up outside it and, with familiarity, she gave him the key to unlock the door. He entered with her. 'Must give Robert a ring,' he said naturally. 'There may be messages which I can attend to on the way home.'

But there weren't any, and he replaced the receiver. Lorna was acutely conscious of him as he sat perched on the arm of a chair, leaning towards her desk, his body stretched, yet relaxed and completely at ease. The light from the lamp fell on his dark hair which was expertly cut and framed his clean-cut handsome features. As he got to his feet he sighed regretfully, 'The evening has been far too short.' To her amazement, he crossed to her side and took each of her hands separately in his, holding them in a strong clasp. His expression was inquiring and anxious as he said, 'Lorna?'

'Yes?' She felt apprehensive.

'You won't back out?'

'I've given you my word,' she said quietly, but firmly. 'And I shan't pretend.'

His smile was warm with relief.

'Good night,' he said, releasing her hands, then added comically, 'Did I have an overcoat?'

'You're wearing it,' she pointed out.

They laughed together.

This, thought Lorna, as she closed the door and heard his car purr away, was Christmas Eve and she was going to be married on January 6th. To *Matthew*. An experiment, without emotion. Why had she ever suggested such an outrageous idea? *A marriage in name only.*

Yet when, both in her profession and out of it, she listened to the sordid, tragic stories; the broken promises, the travesty of what passed for love; wasn't there sanity in this pattern? As she got into bed a feeling of satisfaction and security comforted her. She was going to be Matthew's wife without anything changing, except that there would not be any more conflict; no worry about his moods, or what he felt for her. Their friendship, professional harmony and understanding, would transform the future.

And then, abruptly and uneasily, she thought of Guy and Felicity. Where would they fit into the picture? When it came to it, did a marriage in name only allow freedom to indulge in extraneous friendships and continue with those already established? She realised, somewhat apprehensively, that only time would answer her questions, and that any kind of analysis would be completely futile. She was walking into a new world and an uncharted sea.

To Lorna's amazement Guy arrived at the cottage soon after nine o'clock on Christmas morning. He was carrying a beautiful floral arrangement and had an appealing air of pleasurable self-consciousness.

'I don't care if you haven't got your face on, or are half dressed,' he greeted her. 'I wanted to be first; also I know I shan't have a hope in hell to get near you today at Gable's End when I come in for a drink . . . You look *lovely*.'

Lorna was in a blue-and-white bath robe, hair pinned on top of her head, face damp from the shower. She stared at him while a dozen emotions rushed up at her, uppermost among them being fear and apprehension as she knew that she must tell him the truth.

He handed her the offering, which she put down on a table in the sitting room.

'Something's wrong,' he said immediately. 'Or have I come too early and—'

'No; no,' she said quickly. 'It's just that I've something to tell you and . . . oh, it's difficult.'

He studied her intently. 'You're not coming to the party today, or to me on New Year's Eve—is that it . . . ?'

She shook her head, looked at him with direct honesty and said, 'Nothing like that . . . you see, I'm going to marry Matthew.'

A disbelieving electric silence followed her words. Guy stared at her in utter incredulity.

'Matthew? *Marry* him! Oh, Lorna you can't expect me to believe that—it was only a few weeks ago that you were adamant that you had no intention of marrying . . . you conveyed that it was the furthest thing from your mind.'

Lorna said, cheeks flushed, 'What has, or has not, been said, doesn't make the slightest difference now.' She made a little desperate gesture. 'It all happened suddenly, inexplicably, last evening when we were having dinner together. I can't tell you any more than that.' She paused before hastening, 'In fact you're the only person we're going to tell, with the exception of my parents; so will you regard this as a secret—a confidence?'

He had been standing, listening, his gaze never leaving her face. Now, he suddenly flopped into the nearby chair.

'Damn it,' he said half-fiercely, 'you could have given me some *clue*—'

She shook her head. 'I hadn't any clue to *give*.'

He lowered his gaze and then raised it disarmingly. 'And *I* was the one talking about love at first sight, trying to convince you,' he said with gentle regret. 'I realise you've known Matthew a short while, but I suppose when it comes to it, there is always that one intimate moment—that *awareness*—' He sighed deeply and wretchedly, 'And last night was yours.'

Lorna felt bleak and deceptive because she could not confide in him.

To her surprise Guy brightened unexpectedly. 'But you're not married yet,' he exclaimed hopefully. 'This may be one of those emotional cyclones and I'm going to delude myself that a great deal can happen in the next few months.'

Again, Lorna shook her head. 'We're being married on January 6th—not confiding in anyone until it's all over, as I've already told you. It's the way we both want it.'

Guy looked angry. 'I'm still disbelieving and all I can say is that it is a strange way of going about things. I, obviously, shall respect your wish for secrecy, but damn it, Matthew isn't a stranger in Tetbury. Speculation has been rife for years about who he will eventually marry, and all the girls have been after him.'

Lorna said, 'Please, Guy, this doesn't help.'

'I can't help that,' he said almost aggressively, 'I just can't *accept* it. Doesn't seem to ring true, or make sense.'

'Only,' Lorna dared to say, 'because you do not wish it to.' All the same, his perception unnerved her.

There was an uneasy silence which she broke by saying, 'Guy? I value your friendship and I'm not going to put myself in chains because I marry Matthew.'

There was a note of aggression in Guy's voice as he demanded, 'Did you tell him that I wanted to marry you?'

'No.' Lorna's eyes were wide and honest. 'Nothing like that has been discussed, but I'm perfectly willing to tell him. I just wanted to talk to you first, once you knew the facts.'

'"Facts",' he echoed. 'It all strikes me as most unusual,' he insisted.

A thought raced through Lorna's mind and she said with characteristic frankness, 'I'm not pregnant, if that—'

Guy burst out regretfully, 'I almost wish you were; it would make all this seem real.'

'Real.' She looked baffled.

'Real in the sense that any two people can find passion

overwhelming in certain circumstances, only to discover afterwards, it was a mockery. I haven't that consolation where you are concerned.' He got to his feet abruptly. 'And now, you know I wish you all the happiness. Matthew's a lucky devil. Don't worry; I shall not hint at any of this, even to him. Neither will my attitude towards him change. But, I must say, that if you were going to marry me, I'd shout it from the house-tops and have all the church bells rung. As it is, I will behave with the utmost decorum . . . No, don't come to the door; I'll see you later . . . and don't look so distressed, Lorna. The well-worn cliché about never knowing tomorrow, certainly applies to us.'

'To me,' she corrected. 'I never outlined any particular pattern for my future. It was all nebulous.'

'Ah!' He stood with his hand on the sitting-room door. 'Alas, *I* dreamed dreams.'

He hurried out into the hall and she heard the front door close behind him with a rather dread finality. She didn't pretend: she would miss Guy. It seemed that she had lived many lives since the previous night.

Guy had been gone about half an hour when Matthew rang.

'The Lacy's baby is running a temperature and vomiting,' he began without preliminaries. 'I'm just going over. Never know with a child. I'll keep in touch and in any emergency get you to put Felicity and Grace in the picture.' He hesitated, then, 'Happy Christmas, Lorna,' he added with a laugh. 'We're never more than a few yards away from a thermometer, are we? But I'll be back as soon as I can, and you come over to the house as early as possible. Oh, by the way, I've told Mrs Cummings our plans. Amazing woman; accepted the news without surprise; in fact I'd even say with relief. We can rely on her, and she won't mention it to you if you do not confide in her. But she might be a good help in arranging your things . . . 'Bye.'

In the space of a second all drama had drained from the situation. Matthew was dealing with facts, and what was Christmas Day when a child needed care? And the Lacy girl, who had three brothers, almost had priority. Lorna smiled, finished her breakfast, pottered about to make everything in order, no matter what might happen.

When she arrived at Gable's End an hour later, and walked into the hall, to her surprise and delight, Matthew stood there as though awaiting her.

'False alarm,' he said cheerfully, referring to Emma Lacy. 'I didn't ring you—I just had the idea you'd be early.'

'You read my mind,' she said banteringly.

'Better than you read mine,' he said as he helped remove her coat.

She laughed at him over her shoulder. 'Don't count on that.'

Their eyes met and their gaze held, relaxed, yet with a degree of excitement.

'I thought it would be a good idea to have our first glass of champagne in my room before the others come.'

Lorna had the instinctive feeling that he was willing her to indulge in a carefree happiness which cancelled out questions, reflections, or conflict.

'Lovely idea,' she enthused. 'How long before the others arrive?'

They had walked into his room and he was already thumbing the champagne cork off the bottle which he had taken from the ice-bucket.

'I suggested twelve-thirty.' There was the muted sound as the champagne was poured into their respective glasses. Watching him, Lorna thought that she had never seen him so confident, even ebullient, rather like a man who had suddenly disposed of a burden. He raised his glass, looked at her with a deep intensity: 'Our first Christmas drink together on a Christmas morning.' He paused before adding in a low voice, 'A very special morning!' He laughed with what seemed a complete change of mood, 'It isn't *all* that long ago since we were celebrating last night.'

She smiled and sipped her drink.

He noticed her change of expression and said immediately, 'What is it?'

'Just that I never visualised myself drinking champagne in your consulting room!'

He laughed. 'If I remember rightly, I was not the most popular man in the world when you first came for an interview!'

'Couldn't stand you . . . but you mesmerised me into changing my mind and now, here we are.' She paused and gave a little gasp. 'Oh, Matthew; are we mad?'

'Quite possibly, but I'm enjoying it,' he retorted imperturbably. 'I don't think I've ever felt so at ease and pleased with life. Nothing to *prove*. Freedom.' As he spoke, he drew a velvet ring case from his pocket.

Lorna's heart seemed to change its beat. An engagement ring would be wholly out of character in the circumstances, and a sick sensation of fear wiped out a former light-hearted happiness. Was he going to manipulate the circumstances so that he had the best of both worlds after all?

CHAPTER SIX

LORNA'S dismay was short-lived. 'I want you to have this as a Christmas gift,' Matthew said. There was a note of confidence in his voice as he added, 'It hasn't any history of broken marriages, illicit love affairs, and was given to my paternal aunt by her father on her twenty-first birthday.' There was a mysterious expression on his face as he fingered the case and said, 'I've only just begun to realise the eloquence of her words shortly before she died. "Give it," she said, "to someone in friendship, because friendship endures when all other emotions have burned themselves out."'

A little shiver touched Lorna as she stood there, and then the thought shot through her mind that, knowing Matthew, this aunt might well understand his aversion to emotion in view of his father's tragedy.

'How strange,' she murmured.

'Yet it seems to embody all you had in mind when you spoke of my future last night.' His voice was low. With that he took the ring from its case and slipped it on her finger, looking at her long and deeply. 'I've always known I could never bear to lose your friendship, Lorna. This is its seal.'

She didn't hesitate as she admitted honestly, 'I can echo those words.' Her eyes glistened as she looked down at the exquisite ruby-and-diamond ring on her finger.

Long afterwards they had cause to remember the incident.

'Just the right size,' she said with delight.

The atmosphere of the room emphasised the glow of satisfaction.

'Almost uncanny how happiness comes like little shafts of light cutting through gloom,' he said as he reached out towards her. 'And now I'll take the ring back until January 6th.'

She regretted its departure.

A few minutes later, on impulse, she told Matthew of Guy's visit and all that had been said.

Matthew didn't avoid her gaze as he said, 'I'll bet that was a shock!'

'To the point of disbelief,' she said frankly, 'but he wishes us happiness and certainly will not say anything to anyone.'

Matthew was grave for a moment before exclaiming, 'I shall be glad when Felicity and Grace know; but we cannot have it all ways, and so much fuss is made over an engagement should the news be broadcast . . .' He picked up the champagne bottle and grinned. 'Just half a glass more, and I've told Mrs Cummings to finish what is left. Harris will be here to help her today, and since he is her brother-in-law, it's very much a family affair. The two daughters help out, too. They have a special celebration on Boxing Day.'

'You'll be at Cornerways then,' Lorna said, sipping her champagne.

'And you with your parents.'

It struck Lorna somewhat starkly that her father and mother would think Matthew's absence decidedly odd, and as though reading her mind, he said smoothly, 'I think I ought to come over to the cottage—whatever time's most appropriate. One would hardly expect a future husband to be missing.'

Lorna listened to him with ever-increasing interest. A transformation seemed to have taken place, all strangeness having vanished. Where, previously, his air of authority often touched the edge of aggression, now he was a man in possession, quietly, but completely in command.

'There's another subtle point,' he added swiftly. '*I* would like to speak to your father; put him in the picture.' He paused a trifle self-consciously. 'And I'm not going to apologise for introducing an old-fashioned note, either. After all, he doesn't know me, and may appreciate the courtesy . . . what do you think?' And while Matthew asked the question, Lorna knew that he would not alter his plans.

'I appreciate the thought, and I'm not a very good actress,' she confessed.

'Since *we* understand each other, pretence doesn't come into it. And from all you've told me about your parents, they are unlikely to have any preconceived notions.'

Lorna laughed and the atmosphere changed. 'They've always feared I'd bring some hang-dog would-be artist along, through sheer sympathy. I *was* apt to pick the hungry type during my student days!'

'We shall have some amusement comparing our follies,' he suggested, giving her a warm smile.

Just then, rather like thunder crashing into sunshine, Lorna thought of Felicity, faintly embarrassed because she had previously harboured the notion that Matthew was more than a little attracted to her. Were that so, she argued, he would hardly be plunging into a platonic marriage.

It was an excited hilarious Christmas Day; friends, patients—some mere acquaintances—piled into the drawing-room, drinking every known drink from champagne to Bucks Fizz and a few innocuous lemonades thrown in. All eyes were on Matthew, and Lorna watched the women cluster around him, holding his gaze and hanging on his every word. Felicity said, moving to her side, 'He might be a film star', and Lorna was not certain whether the remark was indication of irritation, or appraisal.

Lorna laughed. 'Doctors can seldom return the compliment. They know, and see, too much! Few of these glamorous females are quite so alluring when deprived of their clothes.'

'All the same,' Felicity insisted, 'he *is* an attractive man; it's that tantalisingly indifferent air. Yet not insolent. One just never *knows* what he's thinking or what his opinions of all these people may be.' She flushed slightly, remembering that she had spoken in the same vein at the cottage, and lowered her gaze from Lorna's . . . 'How do you think Grace is looking today?'

'Still tired, but making a valiant effort to keep up the Christmas spirit.'

'Ah! There's Guy,' Felicity cried eagerly. 'Looks pretty solemn. Hope he hasn't lost a patient.'

Guy's gaze went immediately to Lorna as though the crowd around them were non-existent.

Lorna didn't move, but Felicity urged forward and greeted him. 'It's a splendid party, Guy. I was afraid you might not manage to get here. Have you fed everyone at the hospital?'

'Yes,' he said mechanically, 'everyone is fed . . . Hi, Matthew; you've a good crowd here today. I swear the numbers increase every year!'

'And an attractive assistant is an added incentive,' Felicity said generously, every now and then flashing a slightly puzzled gaze in Matthew's direction as though trying to sum him up, and finding him more mysterious than usual. At last she said with bold assessment, 'You look very pleased with yourself today, Matthew! Haven't been left a fortune by any chance?'

'Not in the sense you mean,' he retorted with a light laugh. 'Perhaps I'm just counting my blessings . . . having all my friends around me—'

'Grace and I are rather new friends,' she said on a note of regret.

'You cannot assess friendship by time.'

Grace added a trifle breathlessly, 'Or calculate happiness in hours. Tomorrow is as elusive as the magic of a conjuror's trick.' She laughed a little self-consciously. 'That is what makes youth so exciting.'

'And you've a lot of youth left yet,' Felicity said almost aggressively.

Guy shot Grace a studied look. He felt that she was putting every effort into keeping up with the pace of the party, her paleness accentuated by the dark rings encircling her eyes. He transferred his gaze to Matthew, but he had moved away with Lorna and was talking animatedly to her. A knife seemed to slash his heart. In a matter of days they would be married. Somehow the fact outraged him. He felt that he had been robbed almost by stealth; that the whole thing was out of character. But, then, with Matthew one had never known. Always the mystery. Yet he was one of the straightest men he had ever encountered, both in friendship and in professional terms. Lorna caught his gaze at that second with a half-pleading little smile. It struck him that she was an endearing person who could defend herself; take her stand in any situation and yet, on occasion, have the naivety of a child. And behind all the turmoil the fact that angered him most was his genuine belief that she was beginning to care for him, and that without Matthew's aggressive demanding magnetism, he, Guy, would have won her. At least, he thought consolingly, he would be able to see her. She had said that marriage was not a cage, which made him more than ever determined to continue their established relationship.

Guy managed to speak to Lorna without their being overheard, while the party was breaking up.

'I'm unlikely to see you again, and certainly not alone, before January 6th,' he said, his voice low.

'I'm coming to you on New Year's Eve,' she said immediately. 'Everyone knows that—'

'But, now—' He looked incredulous.

'I told you I wasn't going to be put in chains because I marry,' she insisted. She gave a confident little smile. 'I shall see you from time to time, and shall certainly be there on the 31st . . . unless you would prefer—'

He asked almost sharply, 'And Matthew?'

There was a natural honesty in her reply, 'I really don't know; we've not had time to go into many details. But I have an idea he's going to Màlmesbury to join old patients of his.' Lorna tried to keep her voice steady; to maintain a natural air, realising that her attitude would always need to be casual, without making anything an emotional issue.

Guy stared at her as if to say, 'This is all quite beyond me.' But he remained silent.

A few minutes later, when all the guests had departed, Felicity sat down on the sofa beside Matthew.

'It was a lovely party, but isn't it a gorgeous feeling when it's all over successfully and everyone has gone!' She made a little grimace at Guy and Lorna. 'You know what I mean.' She gave a little laugh. 'I must say you'll be pretty busy this year, judging by the babies that are on the way. Profitable patients!' Her gaze turned to Grace in that moment, and it was as if she were suddenly remembering her own past and all that Matthew had done to help her. One day she would tell Grace; she didn't like secrets . . .

'You're coming over to us tomorrow,' she said to Matthew as, later, they went into the dining room and he began to carve the turkey.

'I want to have a word with you about that,' he said, 'when we've settled down.'

Felicity said, almost immediately they began the meal, 'Matthew, what did you mean when you said you would have a word with me about tomorrow?' Her brows puckered and she began to eat mechanically.

'Tomorrow is the only day I shall have the opportunity of meeting Lorna's parents,' he said factually. His voice was pleasant, but precise. 'The evening strikes me as being a good time, and will give me the day at Cornerways . . .'

Lorna laughed. 'And we shall have disposed of all the domestic-cum-family talk by then . . . Drinks and snacks. About six?' As she spoke, Lorna felt the curious thrill of independence; she could make suggestions without apprehension.

Grace said, shooting Felicity what appeared to be a warning glance, 'We certainly couldn't expect Matthew to remain the whole day at Cornerways . . . Are your parents staying long, Lorna?'

'Just a flying visit; going back in the late afternoon the following day. Their social engagements fill their diaries, and they go out far more than I. You must meet them when they come to the cottage next time. We could arrange—' She stopped. *She would be married then*. Her gaze went to Matthew and a smile hovered about his lips in understanding.

Felicity made no comment. There was a sudden silence. Felicity did not take her gaze from Matthew's face, and apprehension lurked in her questioning expression.

Lorna greeted her parents, Jim and Judy, the following morning with delight. They had an air of sustained gaiety and happiness about them, and always greeted her as though they had seen her yesterday.

'We left early,' Jim said as the clock chimed eleven.

'You always leave early,' Lorna chuckled. 'You and Judy must have been premature babies!' She added with a grin, 'And don't make any excuses because you've almost missed Christmas.'

Lorna thought, as she spoke, how attractive her mother looked in her sable coat, a scarlet-and-blue scarf tied expertly around her neck. She was only twenty-two years older than Lorna, and Lorna always felt that *she* was the mother. For all that, Lorna knew that she had a staunch ally who would understand even the most extravagant behaviour and mistakes. But would she understand the secrecy of marriage to a stranger, when there would appear to be no need whatsoever for any concealment?

'Just as long as we don't become premature geriatrics!' Jim said. He was a tall, slim, amusing man who adored his wife and found each day an adventure. His aim in life was to retire early, and travel at his own pace in peaceful extravagance.

They filled the sitting-room with cases, and a hamper from a well-known store. When without fuss they had taken possession of their bedroom, talking blithely as they did so, Lorna called out, '*Coffee!*'

'Don't tell me you have Sunday opening hours?' Jim replied.

'You're incorrigible,' Lorna retorted.

He came downstairs at that moment and she put her arms around his neck, gave him a kiss on the cheek and said, 'It's so good to see you.'

'And you're happy here still?'

'Of course. Why?'

'Just a solemn look behind the smile.'

She moved away with a laugh. 'You're the most infuriating father; you behave like a teenager part of the time, and then suddenly turn into some old owl!'

'You can say that again,' Judy exclaimed as she joined them.

Jim made for the hamper and removed a bottle of champagne which had been in an iced cylinder during its journey. His face was creased into a smile and he looked like a man who had come in glowing from a five mile walk, instead of a car journey from London.

Lorna thought of Matthew and the evening. There was champagne already laid on for that, but she could not tell them she would prefer to wait for an event which was, at the moment, a secret.

The cork made a discreet pop, the glasses were filled; they drank and smiled.

'Boxing Day's better than all the rest of it,' Jim said stoutly, 'when one can spend it with a daughter . . . You look different, somehow, Lorna. Less nervy; bit mysterious, though.'

'You've been analysing me from the moment you arrived,' she chided.

'At least I'm concentrating on an intelligent person . . . I take it we're going to meet Dr Thornton? Analysing *him* will probably be more difficult!'

'You've said very little about him,' Judy exclaimed.

'He's coming for drinks and a snack tonight, so you'll be able to make your own judgment,' Lorna said, trying to keep her voice steady.

'I've always imagined him to be an austere man,' Judy said.

'He's not easy to describe,' Lorna said evasively, realising that she had told them nothing tangible about Matthew. *Tangible*. The word caught her imagination, and that made the present situation even more fantastic.

Matthew arrived promptly at six and at the sight of him, Judy drew in her breath a trifle, for he seemed far more attractive and magnetic than she had envisaged. His deep voice appealed to her, and she perceived that it was more his personality than his actual looks that made him stand out and dominate the scene.

But while it was normally impossible to be reserved with Jim and Judy, a moment of silence fell before Matthew said, 'Could I have a word with you, Mr—'

'Jim,' came the correction.

Judy and Lorna went out into the kitchen, busying

themselves with various dishes and adding a little garnish here and there. Normally, Judy would have chattered; now she was silent until, at last, Jim called out and they rejoined Matthew.

'You won't believe it,' Jim said to Judy.

Lorna could not stand the sustained suspense and said, 'Matthew and I are going to be married.' With that she moved to Matthew's side and smiled up at him in understanding.

'Oh!' Judy gasped. 'I couldn't be more pleased! If you're as happy as Jim and I, then that is the most I can possibly wish you. Marriage is terrific, once the two people have mastered the art of understanding each other.'

'Friendship,' Matthew said quietly, 'is the foundation . . . Thank you for being . . . well,' he laughed, 'the word is still *understanding*.'

It was a happy, relaxed, evening. Conversation flowed; discussion broadened as Matthew said that Lorna would become his professional partner as well as his wife, as soon as it could be arranged.

'Ah, but you've another shock coming,' Lorna warned them lightly.

'We're not easily shockable,' Judy said, prepared for anything.

'We're going to be married on January 6th; we'd like you to come to the wedding which will be in a register office. Only one other person knows about it, but we couldn't leave you out. Will you come down and be witnesses?'

Jim and Judy's eyes met. 'Of course,' they said in unison.

'And you won't be having any honeymoon?' Judy

suggested intuitively, her voice smooth and easy.

'No; we shall go straight back to Gable's End. We just don't want any fuss.'

'You are very perceptive, Judy,' Matthew exclaimed, slightly abashed as he gave her an appreciative smile.

'I believe in people doing precisely as they wish: they know their own business best.'

And so the arrangements were amicably settled. Jim and Judy would drive down on January 5th, stay the night at the cottage and, after the wedding and meeting a few friends, would go on to Malmesbury to business colleagues of Jim's, where they had an invitation to stay overnight at any time.

Lorna went out into the hall to see Matthew off just before midnight.

'I'm a singularly lucky man,' he said, looking down into Lorna's eyes. 'Not only an exceptional future wife, but delightful in-laws. I must admit that I wondered if they might take a rather jaundiced view of the haste with which we've gone into this.' His mood changed for a second as a grave expression saddened his face. 'I'm sorry I haven't any relatives to share in this.' He paused and sighed. 'But then, that might spare you any problems.'

'I hadn't thought about it,' Lorna assured him. 'And I was pretty certain of my parents' attitude; they've never interfered.'

Matthew opened the front door. 'Thank you, Lorna,' he said gently, 'for a splendid evening.' He left, looking a pleased and satisfied man.

It was when Jim and Judy were settled in bed that night that Jim asked tentatively, 'What do you think of all this?'

'Well, to begin with, I like him. It was a happy evening.' She gave a little laugh. 'At least we've none of his relatives to cope with; and Lorna will be spared any possible mother-in-law problems.' She paused, a faintly puzzled expression on her face.

'But—what?' Jim prompted knowingly.

'Lorna never once used an endearment when speaking to him, nor he to her. They seemed more like two very good friends than an engaged couple.'

'Probably self-consciousness and nervousness, or both. Besides, you are an incorrigible romantic!' He added reasonably, 'And don't forget that they are two people already working together and he is in command. They are likely to have a far more basic mutual understanding than most.'

Judy nuzzled her head on his shoulder.

'Of course, you're right,' she agreed. 'I suppose, if I'm honest, I'd secretly looked forward to Lorna having a romantic wedding with all the trimmings—like we did. Ah well, she's a young bride—'

'I know,' he interrupted, 'and *you* want to be a young grandmother! That's what's been in your mind.'

She didn't deny it.

'Grandchildren will be wonderful.' Her voice was happy and eager.

Jim chuckled. 'If Matthew and Lorna are as quick at producing offspring as they are at getting married, you shouldn't have to wait too long!'

'They'll probably have a honeymoon in the spring,' she said disjointedly, but hopefully.

'I suppose,' Jim said wryly, 'there could be worse things than their present set-up with one's housekeeper, daily and Harris keeping vigil.'

'*They* won't be in the bedroom,' Judy emphasised.

Jim's arms tightened around her with gentleness. Neither laughed, each troubled in a way that could not be defined or explained, yet knowing that wisdom counselled silence.

Lorna awakened on her wedding morning after a restless night, and faced up to doubt, anxiety and a jumble of emotions, her own words echoing in her brain disturbingly: '*You know you are a man who ought to have an experimental marriage—one that protects you from emotion and is purely platonic.*'

How much further from her own idea of marriage was that? And yet, even on those terms, she had agreed to become his wife. Incidents rushed back; his giving her the ring. Later she would be wearing it . . . What kind of wedding ring had he chosen? And what were Jim and Judy feeling?

Judy managed to be alone with her for a few seconds before they set off for the register office and, slipping an arm about her shoulders, said, 'I'm not going to upset us both, darling, by stating the obvious. Be happy; and remember that you have a couple of crazy parents if you should ever need them.'

'I don't feel quite real,' Lorna said; 'but while you and Jim are in the world, I know I shall never be alone.' She forced a laugh. 'I have an idea that Matthew will make an extraordinary husband!'

Judy, also, forced a smile.

'No accounting for love . . . but Jim and I will give it a good reference!'

Lorna went through the brief service as though living in a different dimension. And as Matthew slipped the ring on her finger, the words that echoed in her head were those they had shared when he said, *'I've always known I could never bear to lose your friendship, Lorna'*. And somehow it was the only reality of that morning. No doubt he would give her the seal of those words—the diamond-and-ruby ring—later.

And at last she and Matthew sat together in his car—husband and wife. He drove smoothly and easily, as though all the road belonged to him.

'Do you like the ring?' he asked suddenly and almost abruptly.

Lorna twisted it on her finger with a degree of excitement. It was not too wide, and was delicately embossed to take away the absolute plainness.

'I love it. I'd have chosen it,' she said.

'In a few hours we shall be able to do as we please—no more deception. Just glorious freedom!' He shot her a smiling glance. 'Now we're two respectable married doctors!'

Lorna wondered if he would mention the actual ceremony, or his reactions to it; but he talked animatedly and there wasn't a trace of nervousness about him when, later, he mingled with the few special guests, each wondering what the gathering was all about. Guy arrived with Grace and Felicity, who said with unashamed curiosity, 'Not like Matthew to have people here like this—particularly so soon after Christmas and the New Year! Must be in aid of something and yet, had it been important, he would have confided in us.' She paused, a little puzzled expression on her face. 'He has been rather strange lately.'

Grace studied Matthew with intent speculation, especially aware of his smiling countenance and ease of manner.

Harris and Mrs Cummings appeared at that moment with trays holding champagne-filled glasses.

There was a sudden silence, full of expectancy.

Matthew didn't prevaricate, but said simply, 'Lorna and I have a secret to confide. We were married in Tetbury this morning, and want you to join in this little celebration.'

There was a moment of dramatic silence, followed by an audible gasp of surprised delight coupled with amazement and a degree of shock.

But it was Felicity's cry that could be heard above the wave of sound.

'*Married!*' she exclaimed. 'But surely you could have told us!'

Matthew didn't give any weight to her words as he said easily, 'We didn't want any fuss and knew our friends would understand.'

Guy proposed a toast, and never had a task been more painful.

Lorna stood there feeling that she was watching a scene from a play. She had just taken the most vital step in her life. She was married to Matthew who wasn't in love with her, any more than she was in love with him. They had gambled the future, making it an experiment which she had suggested, without dreaming of being involved. Well, now she was Mrs Thornton, and it suddenly seemed to bolster her courage and give her power. She could not begin to worry what other women's feelings for Matthew were; she was already used to their crushes, even their blatant attraction for him. Sub-consciously she fingered her wedding ring, and at that moment his gaze met hers from the near distance. He might have reached out and kissed her cheek in friendship, as he moved to her side and smiled down at her, aware that all eyes were upon them.

Felicity and Grace were the last to leave, and Felicity said almost appealingly, 'We shall still all see each other . . . I mean—'

'Our being married will not make any difference where friendship is concerned,' Matthew insisted. 'Work will be our master during these next months, and I know,' he said to Grace, 'that Guy wants you to have a check-up—'

'Oh, *please*,' she said genuinely, 'not my health on your wedding day!' With that, she leaned forward and gave him a quick light kiss. 'All happiness,' she whispered. She repeated the gesture to Lorna. Felicity put one hand on Matthew's shoulder and one on Lorna's. 'Bless you both,' she said tremulously, and moved quickly away.

Matthew gave a relieved sigh as the front door shut.

'I'm hungry and thirsty,' he said with a grin. 'I only had a sip of champagne . . . Ah, Harris—' as Harris crossed the hall— 'collect some of the canapes and see that there's a bottle in the ice-bucket. We'll have it in the study—away from the debris.'

'I'll join you there in a few minutes,' Lorna said, moving towards the stairs.

Upstairs, Lorna hardly saw the large, attractively-furnished bedroom as she slipped into the bathroom. Her movements were mechanical. Mrs Cummings had unpacked, and the large cupboards were neatly stacked with Lorna's personal things. It was like taking posses-sion of an hotel room, Lorna thought, as she sat down at the dressing-table to repair her make-up. She could see the large double bed through the looking-glass. It was brass, attractively shaped and with a pink cover and overlay of lace. The carpet was dove grey, and a writing-desk and chair, together with a damask-covered armchair, completed the picture. It was, she realised, a world in itself. A white television fitted neatly into a corner to give perfect viewing. And while she had explored it all before, only now did it register—as hers.

She was aware that time was rushing by, and hurried to the door, catching a glimpse of herself in the glass panels of the cupboards. Her cream-and-cherry suit looked smart without being gaudy, because the use of colour was discreet.

Matthew stood awaiting her in the study without any apparent impatience. The house was suddenly still, but outside the wind had started tearing through the trees, and whining around the walls. A log fire burnt red hot, and spluttered.

'First things first,' Matthew said before she could sit down.

He removed the diamond-and-ruby ring from its case, took her hand, and slipped the ring on her finger.

'I wanted you to have this when all the excitement was over, and we could be together in our own home.'

Lorna was conscious of her heart quickening its beat at the sound of his words. A lump rose in her throat.

His eyes met hers for a fraction of a second before he slipped the ring on top of her wedding ring, holding her hand gently, saying gravely, 'I'd like you to make me a promise, Lorna: if ever you should want to end our relationship, all you have to do is give these rings back to me. I shall understand, and not question.'

A little shudder went over her as he removed his hand, and she said simply, 'I promise.'

He stood in silence for a second, his back to the fire. '*Friendship*,' he said in a low deep voice. 'Oh, the peace of it. Thank you for making this day possible.'

'I just pray that time will prove me right.'

'It will.' He laughed a little self-consciously. 'I've become far too polite, haven't I?'

'I think you are seeing yourself, and life, as you wish both to be, Dr Thornton,' she said, half-joking, but with a note of perception in her voice.

'And you're becoming facetious, Mrs Thornton,' he commented, half-teasingly.

'Is that surprising in the circumstances?'

His voice sharpened, 'Meaning that you cannot take all this seriously?' There was a dark inquiring expression in his voice.

'Not necessarily; merely that one has to get adjusted.'

They sat down in the studded blue hide chairs. A dark sapphire carpet covered the floor and, here and there, ornaments with touches of cornflower provided a light relief. Signed prints, mostly landscapes, adorned the walls, and an oil painting of Matthew's father stood impressively above the chimney-piece. The first buds of daffodils filled a copper urn, given importance by delicate greenery.

Matthew took the champagne from the bucket. 'We seem to have been drinking this in unusually large amounts,' he laughed, 'yet, actually, we only really did justice to it on Christmas Eve! Let's make up for it now,' he added as he handed her the beautifully-cut tulip glass.

'To companionship and understanding,' he said, meeting and holding her gaze. 'Until now, this room has been completely empty; now suddenly, it is alive . . . *home*.'

'I like this room,' Lorna said with emphasis. 'The bookcases.' She paused and then looked up at the painting.

'I haven't felt it necessary to tell you who that is,' Matthew said, and sighed. 'Wish to God he were here.'

Lorna felt a strange uncanny sensation.

'A fine face,' she said gently, 'and there's a great resemblance.' She paused a little dramatically. 'Interesting,' she murmured. 'Had he been here now, I most certainly should not be with you.'

'By what devious means do you reach that conclusion?' Matthew demanded.

'Simply that your views on marriage would have been vastly different; you would have accepted emotion and all the things you now ridicule, as being part of normal everyday life. No experiment would have been needed.'

He looked abashed.

'You make me seem eccentric—odd.' He spoke as though he didn't like the idea.

'Unconventional and original,' she corrected.

He looked at her earnestly, suddenly troubled. 'And do you see yourself like that, or merely as someone who has gone along with an experiment?'

'I fit into all those categories.' She stretched her legs out in front of the fire, sipped her champagne. 'I also feel at home,' she added honestly.

'As though you belong here,' he suggested seriously.

She looked pensive before replying, 'Yes; that's it . . . No pretence, Matthew.'

'No, thank God. I didn't realise how important a wife could be. Is there anything extra you want in your room?' he asked as though avoiding further discussion. 'Things brought over from the cottage?'

'I'd love some bookshelves built into the alcoves beside the cupboards . . . I really haven't thought about actual furniture from the cottage.'

'Well, so far as the bookshelves are concerned, I'll get Harris on to them tomorrow. I leave it to you to tell him exactly what you want. You've already got a rapport with Mrs Cummings, so that's another possible worry off my shoulders.' He looked at her intently, 'And if you think the house looks shabby anywhere, just say so. I haven't had any enthusiasm to think of decorating, or furnishings . . . and while we're being thoroughly practical, I've opened a joint account so that you won't have to ask for anything. Professionally, things will go on the same, and I'll set the partnership in motion.'

'This seems a very luxurious experiment—a very generous friendship. Thank you.'

He changed the subject abruptly, dragged back to his work. 'Would you mind coming over to see Mrs Willis in a little while?'

'The ischaemic heart case?' Lorna didn't seem surprised.

'She hasn't long, and at eighty-two . . . they notice; and she'll hear we've been married—'

'I think it's a lovely thought,' Lorna exclaimed, choked.

He sighed, a grateful contented smile.

'Is there anything you'd like to do—anywhere you'd like to go this evening?' he asked suddenly.

'To be honest—yes.'

'What?' He was half-apprehensive.

'When we've seen Mrs Willis, I'd like to come back

and settle in over the fire. Play some favourite records. I happen to know Mrs Cummings has prepared a special meal.'

Lorna could never recall a more delighted expression transforming his face.

'That would be splendid!—From the sound of it we're in for a pretty foul night.' His smile broadened. 'I'm glad you like music . . . do you play?'

'Yes,' she said modestly. 'My teacher had ambitions for me . . . Do you?'

'As far as simple classics . . . Now I think we'll get that visit over, and for goodness sake,' he said protectively, 'put on your fur coat.'

'Giving orders already,' she quipped.

There was no strangeness. They looked at each other and then his gaze went to her wedding finger, his words echoing and awakening emotion: *'I'd like you to make me a promise, Lorna—if ever you should want to end our relationship, all you have to do is to give these rings back to me.'*

CHAPTER SEVEN

EVERY moment, every incident, was etched upon Lorna's memory whenever she recalled her wedding day, during the years. The visit to Mrs Willis which seemed to revive and rejoice her a matter of hours before she died. The return to Gable's End; the comfort and leisure of showering and changing into a casual dress. And as she stood appraising her surroundings, a knock at the door sent her heart racing.

Matthew came in wearing dark green cord trousers and a navy ribbed sweater. 'Oh! I hoped you'd change,' he said. 'It's a relief after all the formality. Not,' he smiled, 'that we went overboard on *that* . . . I was thinking of your shelves. I'm a pretty hopeless interior decorator!' But he saw immediately how the wall receded from the cupboards, providing an ideal site for bookshelves.

He moved and stood beside her, observing her loose peacock-blue cashmere sweater with touches of white at the neck and waist. Their gaze met in the looking-glasses. 'Strange,' he said, 'how just your presence here brings this place to life. The atmosphere, and that faint but alluring scent.'

She stared at him almost aghast. This was *Matthew* talking, treating her with ease and complete lack of tension, yet not making her feel any the less womanly for all that, or introducing any sexual overtones.

'The bed's antique,' he said naturally. 'Out of my

aunt's house. I liked it, and felt that it looked right in this room.'

'It's a large bed and a large suite,' Lorna exclaimed.

'When I bought this house I had a partner in mind. One living in, and I allowed for his comfort.'

'Not realising the "he" would be a female!' Lorna said, half-laughing.

He shook his head. 'Certainly not that.'

His presence didn't make her feel in the least awkward and she gave no impression that she wanted him to leave. They walked to the door together and he opened it to let her pass into a wide corridor furnished with a tall Regency chair and an antique table, on which stood a large bowl of flowers. She noticed two doors on the left, and then, a little lower down, an L-shaped turning.

'My domain is along there,' he explained. 'I had it built on. Space and privacy, are great assets.' There was a look of satisfaction on his face.

Lorna realised how far apart their respective rooms were and, in the circumstances, was glad; it emphasised the reality of their relationship and was in accord with friendship. They walked down the staircase together, and a chink in the curtains at the hall window gave a glimpse of falling snow. Lorna ran ahead of him and pressed her nose against the leaded panes the better to see.

'*Snow!*' she said like an excited child. 'Oh, Matthew; isn't it beautiful—' She pulled herself up sharply, adding, 'But not if you're called out in it!'

'I'll put up with that in order to see the pleasure on your face,' he said.

'No one about, either,' she said, appreciating his words. Then, 'Br-r-rh, it's cold.'

They went back to the study and settled in what became their respective chairs.

Mrs Cummings came in and asked if Matthew would open the wine. It had been out of the cellar for the right length of time and now needed to breathe. She spoke with pride and authority, absorbing all that Matthew had taught her.

Matthew took the bottle of Chateau Margaux and uncorked it, sniffed, and said, 'Put it on the dining-room table. It's fine.'

'Dinner at about eight-fifteen?' Mrs Cummings stood there, feeling a little unreal and yet delighted to see Lorna sitting so relaxed in the once-empty chair.

Matthew looked at Lorna.

'Perfect,' she said. 'Is it still snowing?'

'Heavily . . .' Mrs Cummings went to the large floor-to-ceiling windows and pulled on the cord, turning out the main light and leaving only a glow from a wall bracket. 'Look.'

When Lorna had gazed at the moonlit scene and she and Matthew were alone again, he said to her, 'Your enthusiasm is exhilarating. We've not allowed it to take any place in our lives until now.' He gave a luxurious sigh, stretching his legs straight out in front of him. 'Now I can *talk* to you; be absolutely natural. I don't have to wonder how you think I ought to treat you. What made you judge me so well, Lorna, that we're sitting here without strain or tension, able to say anything we please without fear of being misunderstood?'

Lorna studied him intently. 'I realised you didn't want the responsibility of emotion, quite apart from the tragedy that jaundiced your outlook and distorted your view of marriage generally.' She saw his expression harden, and added quickly, 'The chances are that had you not divorced yourself from all normal sexuality, you'd have been a philanderer, indulging in all manner of excesses!'

There was a moment of almost staggered silence.

'I suppose that's a fair enough assessment in the circumstances,' he agreed. 'The truth can sometimes prove our greatest deception. How much do we know about ourselves, Lorna?'

'A dangerous question.' She met his gaze. 'The cliché about ignorance and wisdom can expose us to a grim reality all too often.'

'As far as I am concerned, this is reality,' he said. 'Freedom to sit here; to look at you and tell you how beautiful and attractive you are. Before, all sorts of complications would have arisen, and misunderstandings occurred. Complete naturalness and honesty are difficult qualities to sustain when a man and woman are working together. Half the time they delude themselves that they are in love with each other or, if not that, then there is a sexual attraction and they complicate things by becoming lovers.'

'You're generalising,' Lorna said firmly. 'Self-deception is part of your philosophy, you know.'

'If so, then you must share it to a considerable degree,' he reminded her.

'True. I'll take whatever the experiment happens to bring.'

He flashed her a whimsical look. 'I'll accept that . . . Your hair has golden lights in it. I remember noticing what thick, beautiful hair you had, when I first saw you . . . don't look so surprised! You'll soon get used to me.'

'And you to me?' It was a question asked light-heartedly.

His gaze was intent.

'Conceit allows me to believe that I know more than a little about you already, or you wouldn't be in my life in these circumstances.'

'You have my spirit of adventure to thank for that,' she retorted with a laugh.

'As long as you don't get too adventurous!'

Sudden apprehension shot through her. Looking at him as he sat there, it seemed ludicrous that he could be devoid of all sexual desire. The thought had not struck her before. Suppose he now met someone and fell in love . . .

He said easily, 'I think I'd better give Robert a ring . . . make sure he isn't rushed off his feet.' He dialled the number and his voice had a throaty chuckle as he said, 'Robert! Yes. Remember me? I hope you're not having too bad a time . . . Oh, I'm damn sorry. I like Frank Phillips, but with emphysema one can't be too careful and hospital is the best place for him . . . So you think we're mad, not to be lying in the sun? If you *must* know, we're sitting over the study fire, congratulating ourselves that we are not in some strange hotel . . . How does Lorna feel? She agrees. Mrs Cummings' dinner will be better than anything we could get elsewhere . . . How about your midder? On the boil . . .' Matthew laughed, and realised that he was hardly behaving like a man on his honeymoon night. 'Yes. I agree; you and Freda (Robert's wife) must come over to dinner.'

He'd hardly replaced the receiver before suggesting to Lorna that she should ring her parents. She told him they would be out and that she would speak to them in the morning, adding, 'Do you like going away for week-ends?'

'I've never had anyone I cared to go away with.'

'Then I shall have to alter that,' she said with a bright smile.

'But not this weekend,' he retorted half-jokingly.

They dined by candle-light, the silver candelabra glinting on cut-glass and cruets. A highly polished mahogany table was exactly right for the large room. A deep-pile rug of sapphire-blue covered most of the parquet floor. The sideboard matched the table and held the entree dishes which had belonged to his paternal grandfather. Lorna took in every detail, noticing, particularly, that nothing appeared to have come from his mother's side; neither was her name ever mentioned.

Matthew poured the wine into beautiful cut-glass goblets, then, raising his, said, 'To you, Lorna, who are allowing me to appreciate this room, this meal, for the first time since I came here.'

He held her gaze deeply, in unmistakable appreciation and affection. 'And,' he added, 'to *us* . . . Thank you.' He remained silent for a second or two after they'd sipped their wine, and then asked, half anxiously, 'Do you think you will like living here? Your cottage had charm and was very cosy—'

Words came naturally and sincerely, as Lorna answered, 'This is already my home—our home,' she said. 'There is nothing wrong with it, Matthew, except—'

'What?' There was fear in his voice.

'The gaiety that comes with happiness, and *life*.'

'My God, how right you are,' he admitted. 'I have forgotten the word "gaiety", associating it with noisy, empty chatter, and guests whose presence meant nothing but the boredom of standing about, feet aching, talking to the wrong person, and weary to the point of exhaustion.'

'Ah,' she said on a note of sympathy, 'there's a great deal more to it than that! Shutting the front door and turning back into an empty room can emphasise the emptiness in one's heart. I hate the kind of gatherings you've mentioned, but when one has nothing to *give* to an occasion, it can only be a failure.'

'I see your point.'

'Which is a pretty good start for an adventure and a new experiment. We can only learn as we go along.'

'At this moment, I don't feel I've anything *to* learn!' he said. 'I hope Robert's midder doesn't come off,' he continued, and smiled. Then, 'What did you think of Grace today? I noticed she was a little breathless.'

'I'm afraid I was too busy being Mrs Thornton to be sympathetic, except to see that she sat down,' Lorna said, and her voice was a little less gentle than previously. 'Guy will take care of her.'

Matthew nodded and helped himself to some more vegetables.

A little later, after coffee and some favourite music, Matthew said suddenly, 'What time do you usually go to bed?' He laughed easily. 'Better get these trivia sorted out, because I often stay up very late and shouldn't want to disturb you.'

'And I often go to bed quite early and watch television in bed . . . I don't want to disturb *you*.'

'I couldn't possibly hear,' he said lightly.

'Breakfast?' she inquired.

'Eight, allowing for all emergencies; the rest of the

routine you know, and we can take it as it goes.'

'I'm on duty tomorrow. My Saturday duty day, so why don't you laze and forget for once that you're a doctor!'

'Marriage gets better and better. We'll see . . . you just go ahead.'

They were aware of each other without unease.

'Then I'll go up to bed now,' Lorna said, her mood changing with a sudden awareness of the situation and of his lean, lithe figure eased in his chair.

He got to his feet.

'You've arranged about your early tea . . . your electric blanket will be on. We'll try to make this a good hotel!'

They walked together to the door.

'No formality,' she hastened as he opened it. 'I know my way.'

He stood looking down at her and then, swiftly, leaned forward and kissed her forehead.

'Bless you for this day, Lorna,' he said hoarsely. 'And for making this new beginning possible.'

Lorna hurried to her room, and when reaching it, stood looking around her, suddenly isolated. Her thoughts were racing. The transition from assistant, to 'platonic wife', brought a strange unreality. Matthew's kiss on her forehead and his words left her shaken, but she realised that this night was the first great hurdle over, and that she had mastered it. No disharmony, no awkwardness, had spoiled the evening.

She got into the beautifully warm bed and had settled down when, almost with dismay, she heard the front door open and the car crunch away. Couldn't Matthew have told her what was happening, since he had already explained that there was a special line on the telephone beside her bed which gave intercommunication with the main rooms, as well as all outside lines?

Just then it seemed that her heart was missing a beat and her nerves tingling. This was a marriage in name only, so why should he take her into his confidence? She relaxed and luxuriated in the soft warmth of the bed, content to accept the facts. It had been a happy day and he had obviously appreciated it. She fingered her wedding ring. Now she was settled; the conflict over. Yet for all his ease of manner and air of relaxation, there was still that suggestion of mystery about him—if only because he was able to treat her as a friend whom he might have known all his life.

She thought of Grace and Felicity, what they would be saying. But her last thought was of Guy, and his words of warning.

The clock struck eight as Lorna entered the dining room the following morning.

'A good start,' Matthew greeted her. 'I hope you slept well?'

'Wonderfully.'

'I had a call: you must have heard the car.'

'Obviously serious : . . yes, I heard the car.'

'Meningitis—boy of five.'

'Oh, no!' Lorna said sympathetically.

'I couldn't get him to hospital quickly enough. Parents amaze me. He'd been vomiting, high temperature; stiff neck, and was obviously very ill, but they didn't want to call me out and had hung on all day! . . . Have we a heavy day?'

'Bound to have; the coughs, bronchitis . . . the elderly.'

'Ah,' he said, 'this is something I've meant to tell you: whenever possible I go to *see* the old people. The social services are excellent, but it isn't always possible for patients to get a lift in—even if they are fit to go out, which mostly they are not.'

Lorna smiled. 'You did tell me that. I liked you for it.'

They looked at each other with appreciation and a quiet happiness.

'Did you miss rushing around at the cottage this morning?' he asked unexpectedly.

She realised that she hadn't, but that she had enjoyed Mrs Cummings' early morning tea-tray, with its delicate china; the curtains being drawn to reveal a winter scene of glistening snow.

'To be honest I didn't. I think, for the moment, I feel that I'm staying in a friendly comfortable hotel, in a rather trance-like mood.'

'As long as you keep the mood at bay when you're dealing with the patients!'

The post arrived and there was a letter for Lorna.

'"Mrs Matthew Thornton",' she read aloud. 'From Judy. How dear of them!'

Matthew said with sudden unexpected enthusiasm, 'How about asking Grace and Felicity round for lunch tomorrow? Everything has been rather an upheaval lately—'

'But we've kept in touch with them,' Lorna exclaimed, realising that she had been looking forward to spending Sunday alone with Matthew. She'd even built up a romantic picture of going out to 'Ye Olde Tea Shop', a matter of a few miles away, and having one of their special teas; the large chimney-corner and hanging lanterns whispering of yesterday.

'Meaning,' he said wryly, 'that you'd prefer they didn't come.'

She was a trifle apprehensive of his astuteness—it was like being under the scrutiny of a microscope. On reflection Lorna decided that it would be wise, as well as enjoyable, to have Grace and Felicity's company. They had become close friends and she wanted to maintain the relationship. If they were perceptive enough to assess the nature of the marriage, why worry? Whatever happened at Gable's End was their business and not a matter to be discussed even with the most intimate friends.

'On the contrary, I think it a splendid idea.'

'I know that Felicity is working very hard for the Spring Exhibition at the Mayfield Galleries.'

Lorna gave a little apologetic murmur. 'To my shame, from time to time I forget that Felicity is an artist. She's always around and—'

'And is not taken seriously,' he said thoughtfully. 'Half the people think that artists and writers do their work in their sleep.' He smiled. 'And it is always imagined that if they are not at their easel, or typewriter, they are just doing nothing; lazing and wasting time! It interests me to see her at work, and I genuinely like her paintings; they combine old and new, and have an originality of construction—versatile. Irony! When she would love to have been a portrait painter.'

It struck Lorna that Matthew must know Felicity far better than she had realised. 'We're fortunate to be in the profession of our choice—without any reservations,' she said, rushing on, 'I'll ring Felicity about Sunday— tomorrow. Can't quite get the days right, somehow. But

Mrs Cummings did get all the Christmas decorations down for Twelfth Night.'

'Of *course*,' he said. 'I must admit that had completely slipped my memory. We are not likely to forget our wedding day . . . I must have a word with Robert . . .' The telephone was on the table and he picked it up in business-like fashion.

'All quiet?' he asked with a faint laugh. 'Mrs *Gibbs* . . . Leigh did a laparotomy yesterday.'

Matthew looked at Lorna as he put the receiver down. 'Diffused carcinoma—stomach. Just had to sew her up again. No hope.' He looked sad and yet angry. 'And she was planning to join her husband in Canada where he has an engineering appointment for two years.'

Words were not necessary and Lorna's expression was all the sympathy needed. They both knew that Robert had been a very close friend of the Gibbs family. It struck Lorna, also, that the breakfast half-an-hour had enabled them to cover many subjects without any trace of awkwardness or dissention.

'We'll meet up for lunch,' he said disjointedly a second or two later. 'I shall look in on Robert and call at Cornerways—save you telephoning . . . You're sure about tomorrow?'

'Absolutely. A quiet drink, meal, and talk, may reduce the shock they felt when hearing our news!'

'I think it was the fact that we had kept quiet about it that was the real stumbling block,' he said a trifle guiltily.

Lorna got up from the table with a business-like gesture as she glanced at her watch. She was conscious of Matthew as he moved to the window and admired the glittering white scene.

'Any visits to do?' he asked her as she reached his side.

'A couple . . .'

'Take care on these roads; patches of slush and then sudden skating rinks . . . urgent cases?'

'Miss Mount—pleurisy. Dry. Could be virus, bacteria—difficult to be certain. I don't want unnecessary investigation. Pleasant soul; has always taken great care of herself. In her seventies.'

'I'll have a look at her if you like.'

'I would like,' she said with a smile. 'Reassuring to get a second opinion. I'll see how she is today. You're a fine diagnostician.'

Matthew looked down at her.

'I'm flattered . . . and now I'll be off. *You'll* have enough germs around you this morning to immunise you for life!'

'A good way to protect yourself, or God help you when you *do* come in contact with them!' Lorna laughed.

'Too true . . . see you at lunch. It's a roving feast and cold. I don't like to be tied on a Saturday, and I'm sure you don't, either.'

Lorna recalled how she had stressed, when agreeing to marry him, that she would want her freedom and for him not to interfere in her life, any more than she would interfere with his. It struck her that he was remarkably satisfied with the arrangement.

Mrs Cummings waylaid her as she went through to surgery. 'I wondered if there is anything you might fancy for lunch—'

'Yes,' Lorna said with a smile, 'anything *you* prepare. I feel suddenly as if I've been moved to the Ritz. The duck last evening was perfect.'

Mrs Cummings beamed.

'That was Doctor's idea; he said you liked it.' She drew herself up a trifle sharply, 'But I mustn't keep you.'

A warm sensation made Lorna's heart glow. And it was not until surgery was over that a thought struck her about Matthew's visit to Grace and Felicity . . . wasn't it likely that he would stay for lunch? *'I don't like to be tied on a Saturday and I'm sure you don't, either'*. The *'See you at lunch'*, could have meant anything. Yet to Grace and Felicity they were newly-weds. It would be unthinkable for him to remain there without her, or for them to suggest it.

She finished her work, reassured and satisfied with Miss Mount's condition; the pain was easier; the temperature reduced. Sub-consciously, Lorna found herself driving towards the cottage. Roofs were still white and windows peered from them in the dormer-type houses, painting old-fashioned pictures as though it was a Dickensian scene. Once inside the cottage, it suddenly seemed like a doll's house and unexpectedly strange. Yet the idea of parting with it hurt her. It had been her first home and it seemed to be listening apprehensively for her to discard it. She made sure that the pipes were in order and that the central heating was sufficiently high to maintain a reasonable temperature to preserve the building and furniture. A curious sensation crept over her as she stood at the front door about to lock up.

A voice called, 'Hello!'

'Guy! What are you doing here?'

'I had a patient immediately opposite and couldn't resist walking across for old times' sake. Well, Mrs Thornton; how's married life? That hooded red duvet jacket suits you.'

'Thank you . . . I can make you a coffee.' The words came naturally. 'Doctors can't drink when the inclination takes them.'

'They can't do *anything* when the inclination takes them,' he said grumpily, 'or I'd suggest lunch. I don't think I shall ever really believe you're *married*. It's as unreal to me this morning as it was yesterday . . . Lorna?' There was a note of urgency in his voice.

'Yes?' It was a breathless sound.

'Have lunch with me sometime—the end of next week.'

Lorna didn't hesitate; she was free to do as she pleased. What use any experiment if it couldn't be put to the test?

'We'll check on Monday.'

'You mean you *will*?'

'Love to. Matthew will understand and probably have a date himself.'

Guy shook his head.

'You two damn well defeat me! I can't come to terms with any of it.'

'Then we'd better not go out together.'

'Know something?' he said abruptly.

'Such as?'

'You've become a very determined young lady recently . . . Oh, *Lorna*. It's hell to be with you, and hell not to be.'

'I must dash,' she said gently. 'I'm glad we met.'

'Not half so glad as I am . . . and you'll tell Matthew you've seen me?'

'Certainly.'

They parted, and as she drove through Tetbury, every now and then a patient waved to her and she became

'The Doctor's wife'. It seemed both remote and important, as though her change of name had transformed her personality in some way . . . *Guy*. It was good to have seen him; and a relief a think that they could go out together without any kind of deception. His friendship was valuable, and yet she knew that she could not have married him on the terms she had married Matthew. The fact mystified her, since she had such genuine regard for him.

When she reached home, much to her delight (and a degree of surprise) Matthew was already there, and greeted her cheerfully.

'Splendid; just in time for a drink . . . we can afford the standard allowance in case we should have any emergencies . . . That hooded thing suits you. Oh, how was Miss Mount?'

'Much better.' ·

'Good.'

'I saw Guy. He'd been visiting a patient near the cottage.'

'Oh, and that brings me to Sunday—tomorrow,' he went on easily. 'There was a bit of a mix-up because, as it happened, Guy was going to Cornerways for lunch. So it became a question of our joining them, or Guy coming with them to lunch here. I had my way, and they're coming here. Did I do right?'

'Oh, *yes*.' She was glad Guy was coming.

'Everything in order at the cottage this morning?'

'Yes; no problems . . . By the way, I've been thinking things over and I've decided to let it furnished—holiday letting in this part of the world is very successful.'

He looked at her, a quiet inquiring expression on his face.

'I thought you saw it as part of the practice, or something to that effect.'

Lorna sensed his disappointment.

'My letting it does not preclude that, eventually. I should never have long lets . . . anyway, perhaps I'm too much of a sentimentalist. I just cannot part with it.'

Matthew held her gaze as he said in a low, disturbing voice, 'I understand; you want to keep your *home*.'

CHAPTER EIGHT

As MATTHEW's voice echoed into a tense silence, the first chord of dissention cut through the previous harmony. Lorna appreciated his reaction, but shrank from its implication.

'My *home*,' she said with precision, 'is here with you. The cottage is my property, which I want to keep as a memento.'

He said quickly and apologetically, 'I'm sorry . . . actually, I agree with the idea of your letting it. You'll have no trouble whatsoever in doing so. I'll put you in touch with the right agents.'

'And I,' she added quickly, 'know of someone who will look after it between 'lets' and see that it is in order for the tenants. A Rose Barton.'

'I know the Bartons; he's the chief herdsman on the Marlow Estates.'

'Patients?'

He nodded. 'By the way, I've a new patient coming to see me on Monday. A Miss Duval—sounds suspiciously like MS . . . and we mustn't begin to talk shop, although most doctors do when they get together, no matter what the circumstances.'

Lorna felt uneasy. For the first time, they were making conversation now that the matter of the cottage had been settled. She escaped into fact.

'I'm going to have lunch with Guy at the end of the week.' She watched Matthew carefully as she spoke, wondering what his reaction would be, but his expression was inscrutable and he made no comment. 'If,' she hurried on, 'we could go through our respective appointments for the week, it would help. We don't know from day to day, of course, but the major commitments give one a framework.'

'Telling us at least what we *cannot* do.'

'Exactly.' She felt that he would be affronted were she even to hint that he might object to her having accepted Guy's invitation.

After the first rather vicious fall of snow, the weeks passed through a mild winter. Crocus thrust their heads above the dark earth, and snowdrops hung like pearls, clinging to the gentle green tendrils for support. May arrived in a riot of colour, the trees heavy with cherry-blossom, mingling with laburnum and lilac trailing shyly behind. Apple trees flowered in a symphony of colour, so that spring became a vast painting across the landscape's canvas which was festooned with the varying shades of green, etched against the blue sky.

On this Sunday morning, Grace, Felicity and Guy were coming over to Gable's End for the day. They arrived unceremoniously, entering the house as though it were their own and wandering out into the garden, Felicity detaching herself and walking beside Matthew. Lorna had noticed how familiar Felicity had become with him since January. It wasn't that Lorna had any the less affection for her, but there were times when she feared that Felicity might get too involved. Yet, as against that, Felicity was equally friendly with Guy who seemed to be either at Cornerways, or Gable's End, as though he had lost all interest in his own home.

'You need more rhododendrons and azaleas in this

garden,' Felicity said. 'I love banks of them . . . don't
you think so, Grace?'

Guy and Grace exchanged glances.

'I think,' Grace said, 'it is a question of what Lorna
likes . . . Can we have our drinks on the patio? It's far
hotter than on many summer days.' She was feeling tired
and wanted to sit down.

Mrs Cummings had already taken out the tray. As she
looked around her, Lorna felt that she was walking in a
dream; *with* Matthew and yet, just then, a guest. Every
now and then he glanced at her, sensing her mood.

'All right?' he asked, meeting her gaze, his expression
half-enquiring, half-anxious. And the question had
nothing whatever to do with what flowers they should
add to the garden.

'Fine,' she assured him. 'I think Felicity is right—
about the azaleas, in particular.'

Felicity spoke up brightly, 'Lorna always supports me.
I'm a very lucky woman to have such a friend.' She
flashed a smile at Matthew and Guy, 'Not forgetting you
two, of course.'

Matthew had an air of slight unease.

'Let's go and get those drinks.' He put his hand on
Grace's elbow, feeling a warm friendship for her; a
friendship he had grown to value. Grace was never
obtrusive; nor did she accept invitations when she knew
that an older person could be an intruder.

Suddenly, dramatically, she grasped Matthew's arm.

'I'm sorry . . . not . . . very well,' she managed to
murmur, and collapsed.

Guy rushed forward, his fingers immediately going to
her pulse. He and Matthew carried her to a chair.

'We must keep her upright,' Guy said, giving Matthew

a significant look. 'Windermere—Nursing Home,' he added for Felicity's benefit as he made for the telephone. His voice was urgent.

Matthew, alarmed, supported Grace as she edged towards the side of her chair, her head resting against him; she hadn't the strength to speak. Her heart appeared to be rocking from one side of her chest to the other, stopping alarmingly from time to time.

Felicity, shocked, almost terrified, held her hand. Lorna stood by, knowing Grace's condition was grave, and obviously her heart.

Grace's eyes flickered open and focused Felicity's in pathetic, mute appeal, and Felicity realised that she would not have any night clothes, or toiletries, to take into the nursing home.

'I'll bring your things to you,' she murmured consolingly.

To which Matthew added softly, 'Don't worry about anything . . . Felicity will come and stay here with us until you're better; everything will be taken care of.'

Grace made an imperceptible movement, but she looked grey, seemingly lifeless.

Lorna now crouched by her side; she didn't speak.

And at last the house was still and empty. Guy had accompanied Grace in the ambulance and Felicity had gone on her mission. Matthew and Lorna sat slumped in their chairs on the patio, alone.

'I can't grasp it,' Lorna said. 'We see so much of this, but when it comes to a *friend*—how bad do you judge it to be?' She felt incapable of making an assessment.

'Guy said she was fibrillating.' The pulse completely irregular in force and rhythm.

Lorna nodded and looked grave.

'Can't tell until they get the ECG,' Matthew went on. 'That, thank God, will be done within half-an-hour at Windermere,' he added as though thinking aloud . . . 'I can't believe it, either. *Grace!*'

'And she's seemed so well . . . I know she hasn't seen Guy professionally for weeks.'

'But there's a good deal of strain there,' Matthew exclaimed thoughtfully. 'Grace is the kind of person one misses.'

Lorna agreed and asked, 'What do you mean— *strain*?'

Matthew answered surprisingly, 'Well, it's obvious that losing her husband is still an important factor.'

Lorna never knew why something snapped, and her emotions raced out of control, as she said, 'With your views on love and marriage—normal marriage—it's strange that you have the understanding to appreciate her suffering.'

One single thunder-clap might have echoed in the deathly silence.

Matthew paled in anger—he met her gaze with turbulent accusation, as though a healing wound had brutally been torn open.

'I don't have to break my leg in order to know that it will hurt, and that scars can be painful,' he said icily.

Lorna felt that she had shrunk and that her heart was thumping loudly enough to be audible. After all, *she* had made the suggestion about the type of marriage he needed, and her remark had taken a mean advantage; worst of all, from Matthew's point of view, he had the example of his father's suffering.

'I'm *sorry*,' she said in a low voice, knowing that any explanation would have been fatal.

Matthew's anxiety about Grace whipped up his criticism as, pouring himself out a brandy, he found an outlet in sudden cynicism, 'And I did the wrong thing in inviting Felicity to stay here.'

'Why?' Lorna looked perplexed and surprised to find that she, herself, was a little apprehensive over Felicity's staying.

'You didn't utter one word,' Matthew went on curtly. 'You heard what I said to Grace, but you didn't even make a gesture. And you didn't add your voice to mine when the arrangements were made with Felicity.'

Lorna felt emotion stir dangerously as she burst out, 'Oh, for goodness sake, Matthew; it wasn't an occasion for flowery enthusiasms. We were, and are, all too shocked and upset. Felicity is fully aware of being as much at home here as at Cornerways.'

Matthew stiffened. 'One could say the same about Guy,' he suggested, his eyes darkening as they flashed his annoyance.

'Exactly! He, also, would always be welcome should circumstances demand it.'

Lorna was thinking that Felicity would be sleeping in the spare room, near her own, and for some indefinable reason she shrank from Felicity discovering that they didn't share a room. It could only seem unnatural and invite conjecture. Colour rose in her cheeks; she felt hot and embarrassed, painfully aware of Matthew's unfriendly gaze as, without another word, he strode into the house and into his study.

Lunch was left untouched and Matthew didn't reappear until Felicity, suitcase in hand, returned from the hospital.

'I can't believe it,' she murmured; 'it's like a nightmare. I know she wasn't well when she first came home, but that was just an assortment of things and she's been fine . . . this is different. She looked so *ill*; half her size, somehow.' Tears glistened in her eyes. 'Oh, Matthew; you don't know what it means to be here—to have your support and the benefit of your knowledge . . . it's her heart, isn't it? Is that why Guy rushed her to the nursing home?'

'Yes,' Matthew said honestly and sadly.

Lorna watched Matthew studying Felicity intently. She looked so beautiful—a dramatic beauty. Matthew—any man—couldn't fail to be attracted by her. And Matthew had been interested in her since that first bizarre meeting. She pulled herself up sharply.

'This is not the way we visualised today,' Felicity murmured, and her voice faltered. 'Makes one realise how foolish plans are.'

'Plans,' Matthew said rather bitterly, 'are our illusions.'

Lorna had a feeling of complete unreality. She didn't quite know how they had become so involved with Grace, as well as Felicity, despite the affection she genuinely felt for her. Just then she longed to escape illness and everything associated with it, and for Matthew and she to be alone. The stormy scene earlier was like a cloud enveloping her in depression and darkness, to which the worry about Grace added further misery. Ridiculous thoughts chased through her mind . . . Moira Simms, and the invitation they'd received to a party she was giving the following month. Moira Simms, the patient who was childless and whom she, Lorna, had advised to go on a second honeymoon and put her husband first. Now she was pregnant and proclaiming

the fact to the world. The thought of Guy obtruded . . .
It would not do for 'the doctor's wife' to be seen having
regular lunches with another doctor. She was glad she
had refused his latest invitation. For all that, his
company was always stimulating and welcome.

He returned later that afternoon having come straight
from the hospital.

'What *is* it . . . what's wrong? I want the *truth*,'
Felicity cried anxiously.

Guy didn't try to pretend.

'Heart,' he said solemnly. 'Atrial fibrillation; heart
failure.' He gave a deep sigh. 'I'm so sorry, Felicity, but
it's useless deceiving you. Her condition is grave, but
there is every hope. We've had the ECG—'

Felicity had got up from her chair as though unable to
tolerate the inactivity. 'But if it's heart failure—' Her
eyes rounded in fear. 'I thought that was—' She couldn't
bring herself to use the word, 'fatal'.

'It means that she will have to live very quietly from
now on,' Guy warned. 'She will be in hospital for at least
six weeks and at first not allowed to do anything for
herself. I'd rather give you the facts now, than try to
soften the blow by dragging it out—'

'I couldn't have faced that,' she said, her voice breaking. 'Oh, *Grace*,' she murmured and there was a pitiful
sorrow in her eyes. 'It doesn't seem *possible*—'

Matthew and Lorna listened, knowing there was
nothing they could say that would lessen Felicity's grief
and fear. Gloom lay upon them all and there was no
relief from that first shock. Felicity had arranged to
return to the nursing home a little later. Guy was, of
course, going.

Meanwhile Grace—oxygen cylinder nearby, was

propped upright in a cardiac position. She had been given Digoxin, an intravenous diuretic, and put on a drip.

At some point she floated in a twilight world between life and death, faintly aware of shadowy figures, like ghosts coming and going. There was something in the deep recess of her sub-conscious mind that agitated her . . . but what was it? Something tugging at her memory, and for a few seconds in that unreal timeless space of grey, she knew that her fear was not of death, but of *living*; living to be a burden to Felicity . . .

The night of Moira Simms' party arrived almost before Lorna had time to realise the month had passed. June garlanded the countryside and roses filled the garden with a majesty all their own. Tetbury lay golden in a heat haze and Gable's End had regained some semblance of normality after the shock of Grace's collapse. She was making slow, but satisfactory progress, and Felicity had returned to Cornerways. It had been an amicable parting because she could only work in her own environment.

'I have an exhibition in London in the autumn,' she had explained, 'and must get back to serious work. I know I can pop over to Cornerways from here each day, but it isn't the same, and one's moods change . . . You have both been so good to me.' She looked up at Matthew and her gaze lingered in his. 'I shall never forget your kindness.'

Lorna despised herself for the relief that surged over her. It wasn't that Felicity had been in any way obtrusive, but that her relationship with Matthew had strengthened to a point when, very often, Lorna felt an outsider. She found her nerves were taut, and Matthew's temper easily frayed.

'It will be quite an occasion,' Lorna said as she and Matthew stood at the top of the stairs together after changing.

Matthew took in the details of her appearance and thought how attractive she looked. Her dress was white, on slim lines, and elegant. Her hair seemed to have cobwebs of gold catching the evening sun.

'Very smart,' he said approvingly.

'I return the compliment,' she exclaimed. 'A man never looks better than when wearing a dinner jacket.' They recaptured the ease of manner which had, in some subtle fashion, been lost while Felicity was in the house.

He smiled. 'All the same, I hate these affairs. But at least it's a bit original to be drinking to a *pregnancy*!'

They laughed in unison. Lorna felt happier than she had been for weeks.

'Pity Felicity couldn't come,' he said as they reached the hall. 'But I understand her wanting to be with Grace . . . The house seems strange without her.' He spoke naturally. 'But Guy will be there.' The remark seemed to follow inevitably, Lorna thought. Matthew and Felicity: she and Guy.

It was a good party. The Simms, Ralph and Moira, were well known in the town and had a wide circle of friends, most of whom knew each other. Lorna was 'new' and welcomed specially as Matthew's wife. One elderly guest said boldly, 'You know, my dear, that we're all a little in love with your husband—such an attractive charming man and such a fine doctor, too.'

Lorna smiled.

'And at seventy, I'm old enough to say so.' Rita

Carson, a widow, was a 'character'—prematurely wrinkled like a prune, with wispy grey hair boasting an indeterminate rinse that shaded to blue slate, but a delightful personality with an outsize sense of humour. 'If he were *my* husband I'd want him on a lead!' But the small blue eyes twinkled. 'You're attractive enough to take them all on. Ah! There's another attractive man,' she enthused, indicating Guy. 'Friend of yours? Nothing like being surrounded by attractive men—and make the most of your youth. Age,' she added confidentially, 'isn't what it's cracked up to be!' She wandered off happily, throwing the words back over her shoulder, 'But I enjoy myself!'

Guy joined Lorna at that second.

'You're looking marvellous,' he said. 'The dress is perfect and there are some pretty awful samples here, I must say! Just come from the Windermere . . . Grace sends her love and is looking forward to seeing you tomorrow evening. She's as weak as a kitten, but progressing according to plan. Felicity's with her; I must say she's been splendid.'

Lorna agreed. 'She and Grace are very close.'

'Yes—there's an unusual bond between them.' He shook his head. 'It was a near thing . . . Ah, Matthew's with the elegant Lydia Benson. I don't think you know them. The Bensons live at the Manor House; father's a millionaire . . . Have lunch with me this week.'

Lorna shook her head.

'Why the sudden aloofness, Lorna?'

'It isn't aloofness, but discretion,' she said frankly.

'If Matthew doesn't mind . . . yours is the most unusual marriage, I must say, in that respect. As I've said before.'

'We make our own pattern.'

'And are you happy?' He looked doubtful.

'Of course I'm happy.'

'There's no "of course" about marriage,' he said forcefully.

'You take Felicity out,' Lorna dared to say.

He lowered his gaze, then said a little unexpectedly, 'What with Grace and her work, Felicity has precious little spare time . . . How are your parents?'

Lorna couldn't help wondering why he wanted to avoid talking about Felicity.

'Oh, they're fine. In Madeira right now.'

Moira Simms, moving among all her guests, reached their side at that moment.

'And you, the most important person here, get neglected!' she said, addressing Lorna. 'I've *your* advice to thank for this evening . . . may I call you Lorna?'

'By all means.'

'And I'm Moira . . . if we have a girl, I shall call her Lorna.'

'"Call her Lorna",' Matthew echoed as he joined them, having parted from the ebullient Lydia Benson. 'What's all that about?'

Lorna thought of Rita Carson's words as she studied him, aware again of his magnetic quality—the quality that had almost mesmerized her into joining the practice and, when it came to it, marrying him. She was his wife and she knew, without conceit, that all women considered her lucky. Which she was, she reflected hastily, trying not to take the matter beyond that point.

Moira told him, 'You have a beautiful and clever wife.' The words were warm and sincere.

Matthew gave a little enigmatic smile. 'I only marry beautiful and clever women!'

They laughed and Moira said, 'I'm so sorry Felicity couldn't come. She's a very lovable person.'

'How true,' Matthew agreed, adding, 'One feels protective towards her.' Then, as though he regretted the betrayal of his feelings, went on swiftly, 'This is a lovely old cottage . . . I say it every time I come here; the beams, the sense of space . . . so many Tudor buildings make one feel cramped.'

Guy had remained silent and watchful. There was something about Matthew and Lorna's marriage that puzzled him. They didn't seem like husband and wife. And he had never before heard Matthew express his sentiments about a woman as he had done over Felicity. He looked at Lorna. What was she thinking as she stood there staring, he felt unseeingly, at a floral arrangement nearby?

The party gathered momentum and by the time they left, both Matthew and Lorna were in a relaxed, carefree mood; and as they went into the silent, seemingly empty house, they were suddenly aware of each other, excitement flowing in a mounting emotion.

'A good evening,' he said, well pleased.

Lorna was watching his every gesture; hearing the low, attractive voice, without taking note of the words. She could almost feel his strength, his power, as they walked up the stairs together, their warm bodies touching as arm brushed against arm until when they reached the landing he continued walking with her . . . Her bedroom door stood open and, almost roughly, he drew her to him, his lips against hers as he cried, 'I want you so desperately.'

His words thrilled her, awakening emotions that were new and exciting. She raised her eyes to meet his dark passionate gaze, trembling as they moved into the bedroom. There, even as he held her, he unzipped her dress so that it fell to the floor, revealing her firm young breasts and voluptous body. His clothes discarded, she reached out and with desire that matched his own, smoothed her hands sensuously over his shoulders. For a second they pressed against each other before sinking into the luxurious softness of the bed. The touch of his flesh against hers brought a fierce rapture which met his overwhelming need. She clung to him with a wild passion that was pain and a frenzy of emotion, until they reached that last shuddering moment of ecstasy.

He was masterful, yet tender, and when finally they lay in the stillness, he continued to hold her, their limbs entwined, his lips against her forehead.

The room was full of the fragrance of the June night, and through a gap in the curtains, a shaft of moonlight fell upon them, emphasising the smooth glistening texture of her skin and the gentle curves of her body. With a little sigh she nudged her head against his shoulder, feeling his immediate response as his arms tightened around her and he whispered her name. No conscious thought marred the wonder of the experience; she lay there, content, drugged with a strange unexpected happiness. She was with Matthew, her *husband*, and no longer his wife in name only . . .

They fell asleep, but when she awakened, to her dismay, he had gone. It was four o'clock.

They met the following morning at breakfast and Matthew said apologetically, 'I'm very sorry, Lorna, for breaking all the rules and regulations.'

For a moment there was a tense and, from Lorna's point of view, bewildering, silence.

'*"Sorry"*?' she echoed, and froze as hurt and pride came to her rescue, so that she said no more.

He began to open his letters as though nothing had happened and Lorna sat there, almost choking as she tried to eat normally.

He looked up and said, his expression perfectly controlled, 'By the way, I'm standing in for Robert on Wednesday.'

Lorna was thankful to be able to escape into the commonplace, and thus preserve a little of her dignity as she managed to comment naturally, 'I've never met Robert Lancing. I understood in the beginning, that you and Guy had a reciprocal arrangement. I've meant to mention it before.'

'Guy's been too busy recently . . . better this way and, after all, we don't very often need any help since our social life is not exactly hectic.' He simply stated a fact without quibble.

A shattering thought pierced Lorna's mind: Was last night an explosion of emotion on his part, stimulated by love and frustration? Was *Felicity*—? She shut down on the perilous idea, realising that she was allowing imagination to run riot.

'Surgery,' she said, trying to keep her voice steady.

'I've Clare Wayne coming to see me tomorrow afternoon,' he volunteered.

'Not pregnant again, I hope.' Lorna's voice hardened. It was a relief to vent her feelings even on a patient. She disliked being at a disadvantage and knew that there was no way she could comment on his attitude and apology, without demeaning herself and being misunderstood. The blood rushed to her cheeks. Last night could have been a bond drawing them closer.

She got up calmly and went from the room, murmuring that she would unlock the doors, and that they didn't want the patients waiting outside.

'I thought we'd go to see Grace after surgery this evening,' he called out. 'Mrs Cummings will take any calls and ring us if necessary. It isn't as though we shall be long.'

Lorna stood poised in the doorway.

'Very well.'

Grace looked like frail porcelain, and had the familiar heart flush on her cheeks which made her even prettier, if anything. She had been up for a couple of hours, but was back in bed, thankful to be spared any further effort.

'Oh, it's lovely to see you both,' she murmured, studying them with deep affection.

Lorna realised that she and Matthew had become a part of Grace's life and was touched by the fact. Did she, Grace, suspect that Felicity's feelings for Matthew were deepening? She, herself, had nothing to go on except Matthew and Felicity's easy relationship, which seemed to have an understanding impossible to assess.

Grace looked at them with envy. A feeling of isolation lay upon her which came from fear of the unknown, and her own lonely position. The idea that she was now incapacitated and could only be a responsibility to Felicity, appalled her. She'd had such plans and hopes for the future. Had she been selfish to agree to share Cornerways? A sigh escaped her unawares. She had been so tired of roaming, running away in the hope of finding solace. She wanted to *belong* somewhere. Since Hugh's death she had been in limbo, her smile painted on, her enthusiasms the courage born of determination not to be a pathetic figure, or a boring one, full of self-pity. There were still so many hurdles to overcome. If only she could control her thoughts, wipe out some of the memories, and find peace within herself . . .

'Is something worrying you?' Lorna asked after studying her intently.

Grace put what power she could find into her voice.

'Being a nuisance,' she said evasively, adding, 'but Felicity is getting a housekeeper with nursing experience to help out when I go home.'

'Yes,' Matthew said approvingly, 'she told me. A splendid idea.'

Lorna's eyes widened. It was the first she had heard of it, and a strange sensation surged over her as though Felicity had become a rival and a challenge. She avoided looking at Matthew; it was too painful to remember the previous night, and his easy dismissal of it.

'How long shall I have to take care?' Grace asked pleadingly. 'I get breathless and am so weak . . . I overheard them talking about respiratory complications. You can hear a lot when you're ill,' she added sagely.

That was true; in an apparent state of semi-consciousness, Matthew reflected, the brain registered what was being said, without the fact being realised by the speaker.

'Take one day at a time,' he said gently.

Grace put out a hand and touched his. 'You and Lorna have been so kind to me—' She looked out across the garden which lay green and gold in the evening light. 'I want to be *out* there—gardening,' she said in frustration.

They knew that she would never be able to garden again.

When they left and looked back at her from the door, they took with them a picture of frailty and pathetic courage. Grace had touched the edge of death and would always live within its shadow.

On the way home, Matthew said unexpectedly, 'Will you be meeting Guy within the next few days?'

'No—why?'

'Because I've to go to London on Thursday to see a patient-cum-friend, and shall stay the night. I'd be glad if you'd hold the fort. I don't fancy the return journey in one day.'

'Of course.' She didn't like to ask who the friend was, but it was obvious that he was not going to change the rules of their relationship. And why should he bring Guy into it, since she had not been out with him for weeks?

They talked fitfully for the rest of the journey, but Lorna felt that she was communicating with a stranger through a plateglass window. She could not relax and was acutely conscious of his nearness in the car, and the occasional glance he flashed in her direction.

Later that evening he said normally, 'I've a report to go through . . . Good night, Lorna.' And with that he went into his study.

CHAPTER NINE

Gable's End was empty and silent the night Matthew stayed in London. Lorna could not settle. Would he telephone? How ridiculous; their relationship had none of those intimacies. *Intimacies*. She shut her thoughts against the word and went to bed at ten o'clock.

He returned for lunch the following day as though he'd been down the road to post a letter.

'Any news?' He looked slightly ill at ease as he spoke, and avoided her gaze.

'Everything ticked over.' Nervousness prompted her to make the trite commonplace remark that all too often conceals lack of communication, 'Had a good trip?'

'Yes . . . Avoided the midday rush. Glad to get out of London. The traffic gets worse.'

'Where did you stay?' She was not in the habit of asking direct questions, but the words came out of their own volition. With her in charge of the practice, and Robert available in case of any emergency, his whereabouts had only been important to her in the personal sense.

'The Portman; on the spot.' He didn't meet her gaze.

'For Harley Street?'

His attitude changed, and while he forced a smile, there was an impatient glint in his eyes. 'Is this an inquisition?'

Lorna, furious, ignored the remark. Her heart was thumping. There was something in his manner that was out of character. A sensation of regret made her feel faintly sick and hollow. It was like watching the fabric of the experimental marriage wearing thin. Emotion, tension and suspense, took the place of friendship.

The telephone rang and Matthew answered it.

'I'll come at once,' he said swiftly after listening for a few seconds. 'Malcolm Fuller,' he said as he replaced the receiver. 'Had a fall; they think he's broken his leg.'

And with that, grabbing his medical bag, he hurried from the house.

Lorna stood there, upset and deflated.

It was a week later that Lorna met Moira Simms in the town. They exchanged a few words before Moira said easily, 'Amazing how I ran into Matthew and Felicity at the Portman Hotel last week—I never meet him here!' She stopped, appalled by her own unforgivable indiscretion as she saw the expression of shock and surprise on Lorna's face. Obviously she had not known that they were together. The possibility had not entered Moira Simms' head, any more than it had occurred to her to question the reason for Matthew and Felicity being at the hotel. The bond between Felicity, Grace, Matthew and Lorna, always bore the stamp of deep and genuine friendship. If anything she had associated Felicity with Guy.

Lorna recovered swiftly and said, 'Go halfway across the world and you're bound to meet someone you know! It is so with London . . . Matthew said that the traffic was worse than ever.'

'Absolutely foul,' Moira agreed, thankful that Lorna had risen to the occasion. 'I'm always so glad to get back here.'

Lorna forced a smile. She felt humiliated and disillusioned. Why couldn't Matthew have told her that he was meeting Felicity? No matter for what reason, he had no need to keep the fact secret unless his motives were suspect. And his use of the word, 'inquisition', only emphasised his guilt. Unless he had something to hide, he would not have minded a simple question. In fact he would have told her where he was staying, beforehand. *Complete freedom*, she had laid down in the beginning. He had certainly taken her at her word. She felt sorry for Moira whose embarrassment at her own *faux pas* was obvious as had been, she knew, her, Lorna's, own betrayal of ignorance. Anger mounted. Matthew should have spared her such an indignity.

Felicity rang that evening. For a few seconds Matthew talked to her, his manner natural, so that Lorna told herself he was the perfect actor. His expression was tender, his voice interested as he listened intently to what she was saying, and then handed the receiver over to Lorna.

'I've been up to London since I saw you last,' Felicity said ingenuously. 'Had to go up to meet the director of the Gallery. So much arranging about the exhibition . . .'

'I'm sure there is,' Lorna said, without realising that her words were abrupt.

Was Felicity preparing her defence in advance? Being honest about going to London, in order to allay any suspicion should the fact come out surreptitiously?

'They say that Grace will be able to come home at the end of next week. Mrs Marlow is coming tomorrow . . . I told Matthew about her—that she was coming to help— and he will have mentioned it. With the best will in the world I cannot work without someone to keep an eye on

Grace. She'll need constant attention and care . . .
Lorna, are you there?'

'I was listening.'

'Oh! Telephones seem to distort . . .'

Was that fear in her voice? Lorna gave a little, rather
hollow, laugh. 'Are you coming over?'

'Tomorrow, on my way back from the Windermere.
You're all right?'

'Fine . . . see you tomorrow, then.'

As she replaced the receiver Matthew said, 'You
sounded very strange—your voice . . . Anything
wrong?'

'Should there be?'

'I don't understand you in this mood,' he said, and for
the first time he sounded explosive.

'Or in any other.' The words slipped out.

There was a tense silence in which they faced each
other, uncertain and bewildered, as Lorna told herself
that he was in love with Felicity and merely honouring a
foolish bargain made as an experiment. He, who had
talked of '*cloying romantic nonsense*'! Nothing could be
more ironic.

'I leave that to Guy,' he flashed back.

Lorna was too involved with her own conflicting
thoughts for the significance of the remark to register.
Emotion tore at her as she felt that everything she had
worked for had been in vain. They had reached the
heights of physical ecstasy, only to destroy the companionship and understanding they had previously built up.
Everything became a sham. She thought, cynically, that
it had been so from the beginning.

But her mood changed as she stood there looking at
him, feeling the fierce attraction of his presence and

aware, anew, of that magnetic quality which had always intrigued her. Words tumbled out seemingly of their own volition and she said with a strange calm, 'I want a divorce, Matthew.' In that moment she knew she was in love with him and couldn't endure the pretence any longer. For a second she dare not look at him in case he read the secret in her eyes. Anger slipped away. If he felt about Felicity as she felt about him, then she wanted only his happiness. Of what use rancour? Dragging in Felicity's name? The jealousy that had shattered her during the past weeks seemed tawdry, and she could not sustain it.

She went on, 'I made you a promise when we were married that if ever I wanted to end our relationship, I had only to give you back these rings—' She held out her left hand. 'You, in turn, promised to understand and not question. Symbolically, now, I am returning them.' Her voice shook. 'I must wear them a little longer for appearance sake.'

'*Divorce?*' He echoed the word as though it burned his tongue.

'It isn't working,' she said, aching to fling herself into his arms.

He seemed to freeze and then relax, as he said with a rather frightening inevitability, 'No—it isn't working. I will live up to my promise, too.'

'We used marriage as an experiment in order to avoid the responsibility of emotion. Now we are presented with the bill. Human nature will not be manipulated, or cast in a mould.' There was a sadness in her voice which added to her appeal and gave the moment poignancy. 'I shall go back to the cottage. The time factor won't allow us to be free until the two years are up.'

And then marry Guy, Matthew wanted to say; but there was something deep within him that could not endure the thought of parting in anger, or misunderstanding.

'It will be a nine days' wonder in the town. Nothing lasts—not even an experimental marriage,' she said quietly. 'Let's keep our friendship, Matthew; now we know where we stand it will be easier.' And all the time she was talking, it seemed that her body had become hollow and her heart was beating in a vacuum. Pain, yearning, fear, tormented her. Again her gaze was drawn to him. Later, Felicity would lie in his arms, and he would whisper the words of love which she, herself, had been denied. A flash of hurt made her want to taunt him because his views had become a mockery, but after all, she had outlined the type of marriage he ought to have, and therefore shared the blame. How long had she loved him without realising it? Now he seemed part of her and she shuddered at the thought of what she had done, the step she had taken. *Divorce*. It was like a nightmare. What was he thinking—feeling? He looked pale, strained and shocked. A tiny flame of anger spurted to give her courage. Why couldn't he have told her about being with Felicity in London? And Felicity, of all people, was involved with him. The telephone call just now had compounded the betrayal.

Matthew said something which seemed to emphasise his duplicity, and bring into play factors which Lorna had sought to avoid.

'If we could go on as we are until Grace is better,' he said haltingly.

'*Grace!*' Lorna gasped. 'What has she to do with it?' And even as she spoke, Lorna thought that Grace might be upset by confirmation of what she might well suspect—that there was something between him and Felicity.

'Heart cases can easily be worsened by anxiety,' he said a trifle awkwardly. 'And she would worry about us. She's counted on the security of our joint friendship.'

Lorna's voice held a note of dissent. 'She wouldn't lose our friendship because you and I separated.' She could not bring herself to mention Felicity's name.

'It wouldn't be the same; the pattern would have changed . . . have you thought of—of the practice?' He hastened, 'I'm not putting any obstacles in the way of your getting a divorce—merely that if we could carry on for a month or two as we are until I can get someone to take over . . . It would make little difference, and I'd not intrude in your life,' he finished, a hint of bitterness in his voice. 'You'd still be free to see whom you liked, when you liked.'

Lorna, in the throes of emotion, had forgotten the practice.

She said with a faint note of compromise, 'I wouldn't walk out, professionally, Matthew. But I shall spend most of my time at the cottage nevertheless. I'm willing to wait as you say. Give us breathing space to prepare people for the break, so that when I go they will merely have their suspicions confirmed. And we can prepare Grace, too. Felicity won't need any preparation.' The words rushed out unguardedly.

Matthew stared at her; was about to speak, and then lapsed into silence. That silence confirmed her suspicions. A few minutes later he left the house. Was he going to Cornerways? A sick sensation, an overwhelming depression, seeped into her tortured mind as she stood helpless in the room that echoed with the words that ended a marriage . . . A marriage they had contrived to suit their own whims, and which had proved a disaster. Weakly, despairingly, tears filled her eyes and sobs shook her. She knew she would never love him more than in that moment.

Felicity felt that she had been suspended in space during the weeks that followed Grace's return to Cornerways.

'Everything seems to be crumbling around me,' she said, looking at Guy dejectedly. 'How much better will Grace get? Will she always have to lead this invalid life, walk with a Zimmer (a frame) when not in her wheelchair, and sit in that high-backed armchair? Her feet and ankles are still swollen and she's breathless at the least exertion. Isn't there something *more* that can be done?'

'No,' he said frankly. 'She's on Digoxin, as well as one of the beta blockers for her hypertension, and a diuretic to take care of the fluid. The muscle tone is compensating to a degree. We're keeping a check on her blood and urine—' He made a gesture and sighed. 'She's really done remarkably well in our terms.'

'I'm frightened,' Felicity said shakily. 'Frightened, Guy. She looks so frail—half her size, somehow.' The words rushed out, 'And this past week she hasn't any appetite.'

Guy said forcefully, a note of alarm in his voice, 'She *must* eat. I thought Mrs Marlow was taking care of that?'

'She does all she can; tempts her with everything possible.'

Guy looked at Felicity and said significantly, 'Grace mustn't be worried—you do realise that?'

Felicity lowered her gaze. 'It's all very difficult,' she murmured.

Guy clasped her hand in a little intimate gesture. 'It will work out—things have to . . . I must go. And don't let Grace sleep too much.'

'But I thought sleep was—'

'No,' he interrupted. 'Keep her as alert as possible. Wheel her out into the garden and then let her walk a little way—*encourage* her.'

'I *try*,' said Felicity. 'I really do, but sometimes I feel I'm being almost cruel when she's comfortable in her chair.'

'On the contrary.'

'I don't know what I'd have done without you,' she murmured. 'I always seem to be saying that to someone.'

Guy looked at her inquiringly, 'And Matthew?'

'He comes in every day. Grace counts on his visits. Lorna comes, too—but not so often.'

At that moment Mrs Marlow (a strongly-built woman of about fifty, with a reassuring presence and ready smile) came into the room.

'I've settled Mrs Anson down for the night . . .'

'Ah!' Felicity said immediately. 'I'll go to her.' A room had been converted for Grace downstairs.

'And I must get back,' Guy said. 'I'll be in tomorrow.' He walked to the door and Felicity joined him, together they went into Grace's room.

She smiled at them from her support of pillows against which she looked doll-like and pretty. She couldn't have told anyone just *how* she felt. Life was a strange blurred pattern, and she might have been wandering in a foreign land. The inactivity shattered her, but she knew that any complaints on her part would increase Felicity's burden, and create an atmosphere of gloom which was the last thing she wanted. Her voice, although weak, was cheerful, and she stretched out a thin white hand in welcome. This was the end of the day and she could relax into merciful sleep—the luxury she craved above all else—and forget the worry that pursued her like a ghost.

'Matthew hasn't been in today.' She spoke jerkily and with faint anxiety. Then a puzzled look came into her eyes and she added, 'But, of course, he *said* he wouldn't be in . . . my memory.' And even as Guy and Felicity stood there, she drifted off to sleep.

At Gable's End the following day, Matthew and Lorna tried to make conversation over lunch. The easy companionship had vanished; they were wary and ill at ease, avoiding each other when Lorna could not escape to the cottage. She found herself saying to lessen the tension, 'I meant to ask you about Clare Wayne . . . you saw her again today.'

'And I meant to tell you: she's certainly learnt from experience and just had a minor problem.' His voice was suddenly natural, since he was discussing a patient and therefore became the doctor talking to a colleague.

Lorna nodded. 'That's splendid.' She was too sad to be cynical, or to wish to prise open old wounds. Her heart ached for what might have been, and she felt ill with a desperate sense of loss which struck at the pit of her stomach, her nerves stretched to breaking point. Often the words rushed up at her, '*I don't want a divorce . . . let's try again.*' And then she thought of Felicity and the fact that Matthew had been to Cornerways every day since Grace returned home. His solicitude for Grace, she argued, did not provide a valid reason for the frequency of the visits. And, in turn, she, herself, had retreated as unobtrusively as possible from the scene, going from time to time on her own to see Grace, for whom she still had great affection. The old easy friendship had been blurred, although she doubted if either Grace, or Felicity, noticed the fact and were content so long as Matthew sustained the continuity. Felicity, no doubt, would accept his presence as a right. Life, Lorna reflected, had become an island on which she lived alone. The only person to whom she could talk was Guy. But he had reconciled himself to the fact that their relationship would not be affected by the forthcoming break-up of the marriage, and had said, when confided in, 'You may be heading for divorce, Lorna, but you're still in love with him.' He had added, more in bewilderment than anything else, 'I cannot pretend to understand any of it, and it is useless to try. I also realise that, where you and I are concerned, it is equally foolish to chase rainbows. You and Matthew are a complete mystery.'

It had been like a door closing, and she had taken refuge in silence, while feeling the weight of sorrow and regret.

During the next few days Felicity and Mrs Marlow wheeled Grace into the garden so that she could then walk a little way. The soft grass was kindly to her feet, and she stood clutching her Zimmer, taking in the rose-scented air. She moved falteringly.

'I'll just go over there by the rockery and pool,' she said ambitiously, when she had become accustomed to the routine. 'Yes; I *can*,' she protested with almost childish insistence, as she moved forward a few steps. In that moment she lost her grip and fell backwards, her head hitting a stone beneath a mass of lobelia. It was all over before either Felicity or Mrs Marlow could prevent it.

'Guy!' Felicity cried, white, shaken. 'You stay with her,' she hastened to Mrs Marlow, and rushed into the house.

Grace lay for what seemed an eternity but was, in truth, a matter of seconds, and then murmured vaguely, obviously lost to her surroundings, 'Where am I . . .? Can't . . . breathe . . .'

Mrs Marlow raised her slightly, knowing that if any damage had been done, movement could be dangerous. She had fallen awkwardly and in a heap, her limbs bent.

When Guy arrived and had given her a preliminary examination, he said, 'We must get you to bed . . . no bones broken.' He murmured in a low voice that Grace couldn't hear, 'Slight concussion.' He and Mrs Marlow carried her on to the bed where he checked that there were no underlying fractures, and prescribed complete bed rest. There was an abrasion at the back of her head which needed only a dressing. Her escape from any serious damage had been miraculous. But she was shaken, her pulse rate raised. She made no protest about remaining in bed which was, these days, her friend. She had no idea what had happened and drifted off to sleep.

Felicity, wide-eyed, blaming herself, said as she and Guy went into the sitting room, 'It all happened in a second; we were there *beside* her.'

'It could have been a faint,' he said, 'lowering or raising of blood pressure—impossible accurately to say. But the concussion is slight. Her breathing isn't noisy, neither are her limbs twitching. She hasn't any nausea or vomiting. All good signs, but that doesn't mean to say it will not have shaken her up. *Unfortunate*,' he said with a sigh. 'And it was *my* idea to get her out,' he added with regret.

'She was enjoying it . . . insisted on going towards the rockery. Her head *is* all right?'

'Purely surface abrasions. The thickness of the plants cushioned her, thank God.' He added, 'She might have a headache and be irritable . . . we have to play it by ear.' Guy knew that even a minor upset in her condition could have untoward results, because she hadn't the reserve of strength to combat accidents of any kind. And the fall in itself—even though she was unmindful of it—was a shock to the system.

'I'll come back later on,' he promised. He looked at Felicity and added, 'You'll ring Matthew and let him know?'

'Yes. Perhaps Lorna will come with him. Mostly she comes alone these days . . . it's only just registered.'

'They have to share the workload,' Guy put in evasively.

'Everything has been unreal,' Felicity murmured. 'I hardly know what day, or month, it is. And the work pressure is enormous. I'll *never* be ready for the exhibition, but that isn't important so long as Grace is—oh, Guy, *why* did she have to be ill—bear all this?'

He said solemnly, 'We cannot solve the mysteries of life; we can only try to save the patients.' He went back into the bedroom. Grace was still asleep. 'Leave her until tea-time,' he said as he returned to the hall and Mrs Marlow joined them. 'She will probably want to know how she got the bump on the back of her head; tell her, or it will trouble and, possibly, bewilder her. Don't want her to think she is being kept in the dark.'

Mrs Marlow gave an understanding nod. She knew a great deal about concussion in all its stages.

Felicity walked with Guy to his car.

They looked at each other with deep understanding as he took both her hands in his.

'I'm so *sorry*,' he said quietly.

Tears glistened in her eyes. 'This glorious day—the sun and blue sky—seems almost a mockery, when she is lying there.' Her voice broke. 'I must telephone Matthew.' She spoke abruptly, trying not to break down. 'Thank you,' she whispered, and watched his car drive away.

Lorna happened to be in the common room when Matthew came in as the telephone rang. He answered it mechanically, then, immediately alert, said, 'Felicity? Anything wrong? I shall be over this evening . . . a *fall*!' There was dismay in his voice. 'How bad?' He listened intently without speaking, then said, 'I'll come the moment surgery's over.'

Lorna stood there feeling a strange churning sensation as though all the pieces of a jig-saw were moving to form a pattern she dreaded. Whatever happened at Cornerways had repercussions in her own life. And even though she and Matthew were about to separate, she felt in some strange way that she would never lay the ghost of Felicity, or hear her name without a pang. Certainty had taken the suspense from jealousy, but not eradicated it, no matter how hard she tried to overcome it.

When Matthew replaced the receiver she said in a breath, 'Felicity had a fall?' The concern in his expression smote her.

'No,' he replied. 'Grace. Slight concussion. Not a good thing in her condition. In fact the worst possible thing,' he added heavily. 'Guy was able to get there almost immediately . . .'

'I'll come over with you,' Lorna said involuntarily, and then wondered if her presence would be unwelcome.

'Immediately after surgery.' He accepted her suggestion without comment. 'Grace was in the garden— walking a few steps. Guy's suggestion. He's right, of course. A little exercise, rather than long periods of inactivity—'. He looked at her half-apologetically as though he had forgotten that she, too, was a doctor.

'It's your surgery tonight,' Lorna reflected. 'If I help out . . . I don't have to go to the cottage.'

'That way we could at least finish on time. Thank you.'

She said as though goaded into action, unable to bear the long drawn out process of waiting, 'I'd like to move back to the cottage permanently at the beginning of next month.' There would, she knew, never be a right time to mention it, and she was afraid to drift any longer. She added, 'Grace's condition doesn't allow for any real hope of improvement—irrespective of the effect of this fall.'

His expression was steely as he said coldly, 'I'm doing my best to find someone to take your place in the practice.' The words were terse, formal and to the point. What, she asked herself, had she expected?

'And,' she rushed on, 'I shall tell Felicity about us. Leave it to her discretion when to tell Grace.'

'I cannot congratulate you on your timing,' he commented and there was a withering note in his voice.

'One cannot protect people indefinitely. I'm tired of the pretence and I'm sure you will have conveyed the possibility of the break to Felicity. Natural in the circumstances.'

Matthew didn't contradict her, just stared as though her words did not sink in, and it was useless discussing the matter further.

As they entered Cornerways it had the atmosphere that comes with illness. A silent gloom mingled with the evening light, striking at normality so that it was difficult not to speak in whispers and look solemn, even though Grace would have deplored such a reaction. Mrs Nilson came forward as they entered the hall, Matthew always admitting himself through the unlocked door.

She shook her head, and focused Lorna whom she had not seen for a little while, since her hours were uncertain.

'So *sad* an' no mistake. Got much better, an' now this . . . Mrs Marlow is with her. She's restless. Just 'ad a cup a tea.' She added, 'I stayed on . . . Nice seein' you, Doctor,' she added, looking at Lorna. Her gaze went to Matthew. 'She's asked for you . . .' With that she returned to the kitchen. Lorna recalled the first time she had seen Mrs Nilson—the drama that had surrounded Felicity and her own intuitive feeling that Felicity was destined to play a part in her life. How true that had been.

Felicity came down the stairs, and at the sight of Lorna said, 'You, too.'

'If it's better for Grace not to see me . . .'

'No; no!' Felicity hastened, her mind in turmoil so that her words were not a reflection of her thoughts. 'I'm glad you could come . . . Oh, *Matthew,*' she said with a deep sigh. There seemed to be a world of meaning in the utterance of his name.

'How is she?'

'A little truculent. Now that she has to be in bed, she wants to get up.'

'Quite normal, even after slight concussion. It would affect her more than a fit person.'

Lorna intercepted the look they exchanged and was unable to fathom it. Matthew murmured, 'I'll go in.'

'She's waiting for you. I don't know how many times she has asked when you were coming.' She forced a wintry smile. 'You're a very popular man in this house—and many other houses,' she said, and walked with Lorna into the sitting room which was bright, almost dazzling, in the evening light; and not even the open windows could lessen the heat.

There was an awkward pause before Felicity began, 'I suppose my mind has been too engrossed with Grace for it to have registered that you—you haven't been coming here so often. Is there something wrong?'

Her voice, manner and expression had an innocence that roused Lorna to anger, but she managed to subdue it as she said, 'Not wrong from your point of view, but I doubt if you will be very surprised to know that Matthew and I are separating and, when the time factor allows, we shall be divorced.'

Felicity cried in shocked amazement, 'You and Matthew? Oh, no! But *why*?'

'Are you suggesting,' Lorna asked, 'that you hadn't expected it as a natural sequence of events? Or *hoped* for it?'

Felicity's bewilderment and distress, Lorna thought, made her a consummate actress.

'Don't let's pretend, Felicity,' she said sharply. 'I'm not blind. You and Matthew—'

Felicity interrupted with a little distressed cry, her expression suddenly appalled.

'You mean you thought that Matthew and I—' She stretched out a hand, her own shaking, and clasped Lorna's with an almost piteous appeal, 'For you to be jealous of *me*. I never *thought*! You see . . . Matthew doesn't know . . . but . . . I'm his *half-sister*. Grace is his *mother*!'

CHAPTER TEN

LORNA heard those words, '*his mother*', in shocked silence before she echoed them as though they were part of a fantasy.

Felicity rushed on, 'We wanted to build up a good relationship before we told him the truth. It never occurred to me how it could be misconstrued. Then, with Grace's illness . . . well, she was fearful in case she might lose Matthew's friendship once he knew.' And even as she spoke, Felicity saw Matthew standing in the doorway and knew that he had heard what had been said.

He moved almost blindly into the room, stunned.

'My *mother*!' The words escaped him in disbelief; disbelief that all these years he had been hating the frail woman whom he had now grown to love, and wanted, as with Felicity, to protect. 'Why didn't you tell me in the beginning?' he demanded. '*Why?*'

Felicity shook her head, her expression wistful and sad.

'Would you have wanted to know her—have anything to do with her? Wouldn't the past, and the unhappiness she caused your father, have ruined any possible reconciliation? You had to get to *know* her.'

Lorna sat down in the nearest chair, too upset to speak, her world splintering around her; suspicion, doubt, condemnation, enacting their own bitter penalty. How she had misjudged them, her jealousy like a fire burning away reason.

Matthew said quietly, honestly, 'You are quite right.' Emotion shook him.

'And now,' Felicity whispered, her lower lip trembling in case she should be rejected, and all the plans and hopes smashed. 'Oh, Matthew,' she went on disjointedly, 'you and I had no part in what happened all those years ago.' She ran to him and buried her head against his shoulder. 'Please, *please* let us go on from here as we are. I couldn't bear to lose you. I've never *had* a relative, someone close. After Hugh, my father, died, Grace and I lost our roots. And Grace wanted you to understand; to be forgiven. That's why we traced you here—came here. If you had not looked after me that fateful night, we should still have got to know you. I'm not a good, or bad, person. But Grace is our mother, and that must count for something . . . *please*.' A little sob shook her: she felt she had been running a hard race and had no more strength left. 'I couldn't bear all this to have been for nothing.'

Matthew's voice was quiet and gentle as he said, 'It won't have been for nothing. I promise you ' As he stood there it was like a revelation. He had been baffled by his affection for Felicity; his concern for her; the fact that she had become a part of his life that had nothing to do with love as between man and woman. His anxiety about Grace, and the strange bond between them, had been all part of the pattern. It had never occurred to him that she had become a substitute mother figure, because he would have scorned such an idea, since he never wished to see his mother again. The pain, the heartache, endured by his father, was not suddenly lost to him; his was not a façile nature. And as he stood there it struck him that he had only heard one side of the story—his father's. No small boy could assess a marriage, any more than adults could decide the degree of happiness within it. Only two people, husband and wife, were able to look through that window and see the true picture. Outsiders saw a façade, and made erroneous judgments. He could not instantly forget the bitterness he had nurtured all these years, any more than he could suddenly change his feelings and concern for Grace. *Grace*. The name had no association with the past, and he said almost abruptly, 'Grace did not use that name when she was married to my father.'

Felicity looked up at Matthew and said, 'My father called her Grace. He didn't like her real name.'

'Agnes,' Matthew exclaimed. 'It doesn't suit her, somehow.'

'Daddy—Hugh—thought she was such a graceful person . . . she *has* grace,' Felicity said simply, 'and that is how it was . . .'

Lorna said, feeling more than ever an outsider, and ashamed, 'I'll see Grace now.' She realised that this development in no way altered the situation between her and Matthew. Felicity had not openly been brought in as an issue in the breakdown of their marriage. But now he had Felicity as a relative; the bond stronger and permanent. It was probably all he needed to complete his life. She hated the cynical thought that stabbed: should he so wish, there would always be someone to satisfy any sexual desire.

Felicity went to her side as Lorna reached the door.

'You understand?' she said significantly.

'Yes.' Lorna shook her head and her expression conveyed her apology. 'Regard what I told you as a confidence,' she added under her breath.

Matthew was neither looking nor listening. He was thinking of the past, and the withering condemnation of years seemed futile.

Alone with Matthew, Felicity asked anxiously, 'Will you *talk* to Grace—she's worried herself sick about it. I don't know how many times she has intended telling you the truth, only to lose her nerve at the last minute. Guy said that it must be left to her own judgment and she must not be influenced.'

Lorna returned to the room at that moment. She looked at Matthew whose gaze met hers without a flicker of expression, reducing her to numbed silence for a second, then she said urgently, 'Grace wants you—' And even as she spoke, they heard a faint voice calling, '*Matthew!*'

He hurried into the bedroom and sat down by the bed. Emotion flooded over him as he looked at Grace's pale face and dark-rimmed eyes. Their relationship took on a new dimension, and his anxiety was magnified to distressing proportions as he saw her in an entirely different light.

'I . . . must talk,' she began earnestly, her expression full of apprehension. 'Tell you . . . the truth.'

He took her hand in his as he said quietly, reassuring-ly, 'I know. Felicity has just told me.'

Surprise, alarm, fear, betrayed itself in her voice which broke as she said, 'Oh, *Matthew* . . . forgive me—please forgive me.' She bowed her head as she spoke, in a gesture of contrition. She was trembling, and he feared for her because of the strain imposed, particu-larly after the events of the day.

'I want you to do something for me,' he said, trying to

minimise the tension and emotional conflict she was fighting to overcome.

'Anything,' she whispered, her breathing suddenly alarmingly laboured.

Matthew swiftly, urgently, wheeled the oxygen cylinder into position, and put the mask over her mouth, sitting there beside her, still, his eyes meeting hers so that she relaxed slightly, thankful, as the time passed, eventually to be able to breathe unaided.

Matthew began where he had left off, 'I want you,' he said firmly, 'to wipe out the past—never to talk of it again. It isn't every day a man discovers that his mother is already a much loved *friend*. Let us keep that friendship, Grace; build on it; make up for the lost years . . . When you are better we'll—'

She interrupted him as she said with a wan smile, 'Dear Matthew—*you* know and *I* know that there is no question of my getting better. I don't delude myself . . . no, *listen* to me. Please let me be honest.' She sighed and shook her head. 'Pretence and keeping up . . . so wearying, not just for me, but for everyone else, too. To accept the truth cheerfully; and to see things in perspective . . . that's the important thing.' She faltered for a second, and he didn't interrupt her, his heart leaden. 'Now I'm an anxiety, and I shall become a greater burden; a burden that will grow heavier as each day passes. You know it's true. Felicity is wonderful, but she's *tied*. Her work and her life, if I dragged on, would be forfeited to me. I dread that above everything. Death is not the tragedy; but *life* can be, in these circumstances.' She looked at him and relief shone in her eyes. 'You're a doctor; you can assess; I don't want any barriers between us for the time that is left. To have one

person who knows how I . . . *feel* . . . Who better than
my own son?'

Matthew tried to speak, but he couldn't; his grasp of
her hand tightened, and they sat in silence in which there
was love and understanding; but he knew, with a dread
certainty, that she was right.

'Now you must rest,' he said, his voice empty and
hollow despite the tenderness. He got to his feet, leaned
forward and kissed her forehead.

'I'd like to see Felicity and Lorna,' she said pleadingly.
'Just for a minute.'

He fetched them.

'Now I'm content,' she murmured, and suddenly her
breathing deteriorated; she began to cough, putting a
hand up to her chest as the pain struck, her lips turning
blue.

Matthew, helpless, devastated, realised that it was a
pulmonary embolism and that there was nothing he
could do, as his fingers reached automatically for her
pulse.

Grace was dead . . .

Lorna lived through the following week in a state
of bitter recrimination. Grace's death, while never
wholly unexpected in such a case, had struck with such
suddenness that they were all shattered. And while,
as Grace would have wished, they endeavoured to
avoid the gloom associated with a funeral, each felt
an overwhelming sadness because she had been
greatly loved. For Matthew that sadness was touched
with irony because he had discovered her identity too
late.

It was a matter of days before Lorna was due to leave

Gable's End for good, that Felicity implored her not to break up the marriage.

'I believe you love Matthew,' she said urgently, having come specially to the cottage where she knew Lorna would be at that particular time in the evening. 'He hasn't mentioned your relationship to me; merely assumed that I accepted the situation. He doesn't find it easy to express emotion. Everything I said about him that night here is no less true now. And there are no shadows so far as I am concerned . . . Oh, Lorna, life is so short—each *day* . . . Grace's death has taught me so much, and makes quarrels and misunderstandings so futile—whatever one's differences. And if you imagine I don't know love—real love—you're wrong.'

Lorna started; inquiry on her face. There was an earnestness in Felicity's voice that arrested her attention.

'Because my life has not been exactly conventional . . . Well, what happened when we first met must have coloured your opinion of me, and—'

Lorna interrupted with fervour. 'No; *no*, Felicity, that isn't true. A doctor doesn't see anything as black or white; or make judgments.'

Felicity accepted that, and went on quietly, 'Guy was the lover I mentioned to you, and when I met him again, I realised that I loved him. If anything, I was jealous of *you* where he was concerned. He knew the truth about Grace and me—our relationship to Matthew. It was a confidence he respected. That was why he became our doctor. It would have been impossible for Matthew to look after us. In the beginning I was an emergency. Don't forget, also, that Matthew was a complete stranger to us, and my interest in him, and eagerness to know him better—the reason for it—must be obvious now.'

'Oh, Felicity,' Lorna whispered, humbled. 'If only I'd *realised*.'

'You couldn't possibly have done,' Felicity commented generously. 'But if all that has happened could bring about a reconciliation between you and Matthew . . . Oh, *Lorna*! Couldn't you *try*?'

'It isn't as simple as that,' Lorna said sorrowfully. 'You can't build on silence, and as you say, Matthew doesn't find it easy to express emotion.' Her voice hardened as she recalled his reaction after their night together.

Felicity looked at her very levelly. 'Pride is no substitute for love; it won't heal any wounds, or ease the loneliness. Promise me you'll think it over? Once you've taken that irrevocable step—'

'I wish I could think he would miss me . . . if only he had made *some* effort to prevent my going,' Lorna said, the words rushing out. Now that she knew the truth about Felicity, his attitude was even more incomprehensible.

'His motives may be as distorted as yours have been,' Felicity said sagely. 'We never allow for others sharing our own follies, or clinging to the same misconceptions.'

Lorna knew that to be true, and Felicity grew in stature in that moment, the old affection surging back, the warmth, the admiration.

'I'm being selfish,' Felicity went on. 'I can't think of a lovelier wife for Matthew than you. And Grace was so fond of you, too. It would be such a bond . . . Guy knows about the divorce?'

'Yes.'

'There has been so much to discuss,' Felicity said, and

sighed, 'that we haven't talked normally about other things.' There was a wistful note in her voice, 'But we've been very much closer recently.'

'Whatever happens,' Lorna said and emotion stabbed her, 'you and I must never lose touch. I shan't stay here if Matthew and I part. I shall sell the cottage as it stands and take a post abroad.'

Felicity met her gaze and friendship flowed between them. 'I'm glad you use the word, "if". It gives me hope that you will never *go* abroad—except for a holiday!'

In that second Lorna thought about Matthew and Felicity's trip to London, and why neither had mentioned it; but she thrust the matter aside. Obviously they had some good reason for their silence, and she could not bring herself to pry.

Felicity left the cottage a little later, standing at the door after saying goodbye and adding as she moved away to her car, 'I shall ring you tomorrow . . .' The words held significance.

It was Mrs Cummings who endangered Lorna's iron control as Lorna's cases were finally packed and ready to be put in the car.

'Oh, madam,' she murmured, tears in her eyes. 'I can't bear you to go. Somehow I never believed you would . . . I mean, what will Doctor do without you? I know it's not my place, but isn't there *anything*—?' Tears rolled down her cheeks. 'You've been so good to me—never a cross word; always appreciating everything I do.'

Matthew came into the hall at that moment. Mrs Cummings fumbled for her handkerchief, gave Lorna a swift glance, and hurried back to the kitchen.

'I've packed,' Lorna said suddenly, nervously, not

being able to think of anything else.

'Then perhaps we could have a last civilised drink together,' he suggested, to her amazement.

'Yes,' she said weakly, and they went into his study together. 'I shall still be working here until you're fixed up with a replacement,' she reminded him.

'I've a possible candidate,' he volunteered, not having broached the subject previously. 'A plump, middle-aged woman,' he added without smiling. 'One learns from experience.'

'That is not only *your* prerogative,' she retorted, the emotion and tension between them becoming unbearable.

'True.' He poured out their respective drinks and their fingers touched as he handed her the glass. An electric shock might have struck her and she spilt some of the sherry.

Their eyes met, warily, passion veiled, as almost immediately they looked away and sat down. And suddenly, all that Felicity had said rang in her ears, '*Pride is no substitute for love; it won't heal any wounds, or ease the loneliness*'.

Words came tumbling out, unrehearsed, undreamed of, as she said, 'Oh, Matthew; would it make any difference between us if I told you I love you? And that I never really *wanted* a divorce?'

The sudden silence was like that before an earthquake.

Then he cried, shocked, disbelieving, 'Are you serious?' His voice suggested that he dare not believe her.

'Oh, yes,' she whispered. 'I think it is the only serious thing I've said since I first met you.' She rushed on, 'I don't want to upset your plans, embarrass you, and you've only to say if you want to go on with the divorce; but I've no pride left, and I can't pretend any longer . . . I just *can't*,' she added brokenly. 'I've misjudged you and I was jealous of Felicity,' she added with almost child-like ingenuousness.

'Oh, my God Lorna; what hell we've been through for nothing!' He got to his feet and almost lifted her from her chair, his arms like a vice around her. 'Any *difference*,' he echoed, a note of exultation in his voice. 'The difference between living and utter desolation.'

She looked up at him. 'You mean that you—'

'I love you,' he said simply, his voice deep, emotional.

'But why didn't you tell me?'

'It's a long story,' he murmured, and his lips touched hers with increasing passion while they clung together as though afraid that some unseen force would part them, before sitting down side by side, hands clasped. 'I feared love,' he began honestly, 'and when you came into my life I refused to acknowledge it, while knowing I couldn't do without you. I wanted to be secure with you— life simplified. And when you outlined your idea of the kind of marriage I ought to have, I jumped at it. After that, I was afraid of breaking my word and losing you.'

They looked at each other with passionate intensity, their gaze deepening until they lost themselves in the ecstasy of that quiet moment.

Lorna broke the silence as she said, 'I felt rejected when you apologised that morning, and told myself that what had happened between us was stimulated by your need for Felicity, and I was merely an instrument. When I suggested divorce, I didn't want to stand in the way of your happiness with her. How ludicrous it all seems now.'

He shook his head, almost appalled. 'I was so blind. Loving you, I realised that I could not just sleep with you in the emptiness of our experiment, and I thought I'd lose you altogether if I rushed things. I also thought—' He hesitated, half-apologetically. 'I also thought,' he repeated, 'that you were in love with Guy; but your wanting a divorce came like a bombshell and, for my part, I couldn't stand in the way of your freedom, either.'

'Guy?' she echoed, shaking her head. 'Never, Matthew; but I wouldn't admit even to myself that I loved you, until it was too late.' Again she thought of Felicity's words, '*His motives may be as distorted as yours have been . . . we never allow for others sharing our follies, or clinging to the same misconceptions*'. And Lorna asked herself if she would ever have had the courage to tell Matthew that she loved him, but for Felicity's wise counsel. The warm glow of gratitude touched her.

'Oh, *darling*,' Matthew whispered, 'if only I'd *known*.' He sighed deeply. 'Those terrible days after I'd been to London.'

Lorna said swiftly, involuntarily, 'Moira Simms told me she had seen you at the Portman Hotel with Felicity. It confirmed my fears, and was instrumental in my deciding as I did.'

'Oh, no!' He looked horrified, and made a little regretful sound.

'Now, my suspicions seem fantastic, but at the *time*—'

He held her gaze with understanding sympathy.

'Your reactions were normal. It just didn't occur to

me. After all, we didn't confide in each other then, anyway. But that was different. Felicity happened to be going to London at the same time as I had to see Andrew Blake, and I enlisted her help in buying you a birthday present! We had lunch together.' He added swiftly, 'I know your birthday isn't until August 12th, but I also knew that I shouldn't be going to London again before then. I'd all manner of plans, hopes, centered around the twelfth; and then when you questioned me about the trip, your attitude was so hostile that I resented it.' He made a little self-critical gesture. 'How clearly one can see things with hindsight, and how blind one can be at the time and in emotional turmoil.'

Her fingers tightened around his as she said, 'It was the secrecy, and when Felicity mentioned going to London . . . well, everything fitted. I ached then for some sign that you loved me, or needed me. I just wasn't strong enough to carry through the bargain I'd made.'

'We were both arrogant to think we could re-draft marriage to suit ourselves,' he exclaimed gravely. 'It was an unnatural experiment and we've both paid for it.'

'If only I'd known you were jealous of Guy! . . .' Feminine curiosity got the better of her as she said tentatively, 'A birthday present?'

'About which you will know nothing until the twelfth,' he warned her firmly. Actually, he had bought her a delicate diamond-and-ruby brooch which Felicity herself had fallen in love with.

'Oh!'

'You know,' he went on as though thinking aloud, 'I realise that I never thought of Felicity in the man-woman sense. I couldn't fathom my protective instinct for her; or the feeling of ease I had with her and Grace,' he added gently. 'It would never have occurred to me to ask any other woman to come with me to buy *you* a gift. I wish, also, *I* had known I was capable of making you jealous,' he added wryly.

They laughed together and then she said quietly, 'Felicity is a wonderful person. I hope she and Guy find happiness together.'

'She and Guy?' Matthew looked surprised.

'I think they will marry,' Lorna suggested.

'That would be splendid,' he said with fervour.

Passion mounted as they looked at each other, all the misery and conflict of months vanishing as he took her into his arms.

'You didn't take off your rings,' he said, a note of happiness and relief in his voice.

'I couldn't,' she admitted. 'They represented my love for you.'

He lifted her hands and kissed them before his lips found hers, ecstasy and desire bringing the magic of fulfilment.

When she drew back, her eyes met his as she murmured with a little intimate smile, 'You won't need your plump middle-aged assistant now!'

'No,' he said, looking down at her proudly, 'I have my *wife*.'

The perfect holiday romance.

ACT OF BETRAYAL
Sara Craven

MAN HUNT
Charlotte Lamb

YOU OWE ME
Penny Jordan

LOVERS IN THE AFTERNOON
Carole Mortimer

Have a more romantic holiday this summer with the
Mills & Boon holiday pack.

Four brand new titles, attractively packaged for only £4.40.

The holiday pack is published on the 14th June. Look out for it
where you buy Mills & Boon.

The Rose of Romance